Kissing Bree

by

JoMarie DeGioia

PUBLISHED BY:

Bailey Park Publishing

Kissing Bree

Book Nine of the Cypress Corners Series

by

JoMarie DeGioia

Chapter 1

Chapman Financial, Boston

Derek Stone clicked through the docs on his laptop, searching for any possible bit of information that could hinder the upcoming deal. Bill Chapman, his boss of three years, was a hard ass and that was just one of the reasons Derek liked working for him. The pay was great and the challenges were real. He'd miss it. That was for sure.

Satisfied that he'd dotted every I and crossed every T, he clicked the docs closed one at a time and turned to face the broad windows at his back. His stellar office at Chapman stood as if suspended over the city, and the spring sky was a bright blue dotted just right with clouds reflected in the windows of the skyscrapers surrounding it. For far from the first time he felt like he was floating. Floating through life, like his old man used to say.

Bitterness bit at him but he pushed it down. He hadn't given more than a passing thought to that drunk in years and he wasn't going to spend time on him now. His father was a waste of air, and he was grateful that his mother had finally kicked him out last year. It had been Derek's singular satisfaction to make sure that the divorce decree was unbreakable.

His cell phone rang and he saw he had a call from his sister. Abby had been nagging him about his plans for months now, and he was happy he was able to give her good news today. Or the hopes for some good news at least. Picking up the phone, he swiped and answered.

"Hey, Abby."

"Hey, big bro!"

Her voice was bright and upbeat, which he was pleased to hear. He could also hear dogs barking in the background and knew she was calling from work. "What's up?"

"I was wondering if you've made up your mind."

He stifled a grunt. "I have, and when I know the particulars I'll let you know."

"I'm not one of your clients, Derek," she teased. "Particulars aside, you don't sound very happy about it."

"I'm not," he said before he could stop himself.

She sucked in an audible breath. "I thought we agreed."

"Yes, we did." He took in a breath himself and slowly let it out. "We're going forward with this and we'll all be happy."

Abby laughed. "Wow. You really have to work on your words and tone, bro. It's a good thing that you write so much at

Chapman. At the speaking? You're not so good."

He smiled in spite of himself. "Just tell Mom that we'll have a place for her in the fall."

"Oh, good."

"Derek," Bill Chapman boomed as he entered Derek's office.

Derek held up a hand to his boss. "Abby, we'll talk later," he said into the phone. "I promise."

A commotion sounded from his sister's side of the call, people talking and more barking, and he figured he was saved from more of this conversation even before Bill had come in.

"Call me tonight, Derek?" she asked.

"Okay." He disconnected and set his phone on the desk. "What can I do for you, Bill?"

Bill held up his hands. "I didn't mean to barge in."

Derek bit his tongue. *Since when?* His boss was never one to knock.

"No worries. What can I do for you?"

"I've looked over your proposal." Bill settled in the chair opposite. "I'm not happy."

Derek sat and faced his boss. Bill Chapman was a big guy, tall and broad, and his hair was still dark and thick. His clothes were Brooks Brothers but his attitude would fit in just as well down at the docks. If Derek had to pick which side he most admired, he'd have a tough time of it.

"What aren't you happy about, exactly?"

"You want to leave Chapman."

Derek kept his expression even. "Not precisely."

Bill blustered a little. "All right. In your words, in a lot of your words actually, you said you want the position down at Cypress Corners."

"I would be working for your son Rick," Derek pointed out. "At the Sales Center. I'd be their in-house counsel."

Bill nodded. "Yes, and when Forbes at Cypress contacted me about the position you were the first person I thought of."

"Thank you." Derek inclined his head. "Then what is the problem?"

"It just feels like I keep losing people to Forbes." A smile played over Bill's mouth. "All of my children. Eli. Now, you."

Eli, his former colleague at Chapman, had moved down there permanently last fall and was now in charge of the Active Adult community. Eli had called him about it just a couple of weeks ago, since the two of them had gone on a scouting mission for Bill together a year ago. It was his call that made

Derek's decision all that much easier.

"This is a good move for me, Bill."

"No argument there. It should be a cake-walk for you, too."

"I'll be on retainer, if you're still sure you want that. You'll have my help on anything you need done, barring any conflict of interest."

Bill waved a hand. "Yes, I know. And damn right you'll still be on retainer."

He felt Bill's respect in that sharp retort. There was something eating his boss though, but Derek wasn't a touchy-feely kind of guy. He wasn't one to pry into the man's affairs, either. There was palpable tension between Bill and his kids. He'd felt that when he'd been down in Cypress a year ago. He had his own family drama, didn't he? He didn't have to mix in with the Chapman stuff, whatever it was.

"I'll go down to Cypress and settle in. This won't be forever."

Bill did smile then, wide and a little surprising. "You'll never come back." He stood. "None of you ever come back."

Derek let that one slide past him. "Then it's a go?"

Bill studied him, a decidedly paternal warmth in his gaze.

9

"You've done great work for me, Derek. I have every faith that you'll do the same for Forbes. For Rick. Hell, for Cypress."

Derek extended his hand and Bill took it, giving it a firm shake.

"Thank you, Bill."

Bill released him and shook his head. "Don't thank me just yet. You've only been down there once and for a very brief visit."

"That's true. What are you saying?"

"Cypress Corners is very different from Boston, Derek. From the Boston you and I know, anyway."

Derek didn't think Bill's Boston was anything like Derek's, except on the surface. Private schools, privileged lifestyle? Yeah, Derek and Abby had all of that. Their family life held a nasty secret, though. All of that serene polish of his parents' marriage only just hid the blight that was his father's true self.

"I can deal with the tree-huggers, Bill."

Bill barked out a laugh. "Oh, of that I have no doubt. You'll have to bring a different kind of work ethic to Cypress, though. And forget about burning the candle at both ends."

"You say that like it's a bad thing."

10

"You're like me, Derek. Work is everything."

God, was that true? "I'll adjust."

"Then have at them. I'll tell Forbes to expect you next week."

"And I'll forward what I've been working on to you. You can decide who'll fill my shoes."

"Son, no one can fill your shoes."

With that little bit of folksy praise, Derek felt valued. Appreciated. Though he might not want to admit it, it felt good. For this next step, he'd need to carry this feeling down to Cypress Corners.

God knew he'd need to keep his head in the game or lose his main objective. He would see his mother safe and well, and ready to start her own life at last.

***

Cypress Corners, Florida

Sabrina James hummed to herself as she took a tray of gooey chocolate chip cookies out of the oven. The table was set. The overhead lights and the pendants above the tall quartz counter cast a warm glow over the light wood cabinets and gleaming stainless appliances. The stage was set as well, and Bree knew that the intended audience would fall for this hook, line and sinker. It was Monday morning, a blessedly typical one for her, and the home was bright and light and ready to be viewed.

"Come into my parlor, said the spider to the fly," she murmured, a smile on her lips.

The Craftsman-style model home in the green neighborhood of Cypress Corners was ready-made for families of just about every incarnation. This particular section of the property took the community's promise of sustainability and an eye to conservation to a new level. The architect and builder of these homes designed and built to specifications she'd never heard of before coming to work here.

The sky was dark this morning, and spring showers were expected. Weather aside, she anticipated heavy foot traffic at the model after its being closed over the weekend. That alone was unusual for real estate sales, but in her year at Cypress she'd yet to find a flaw in the business plan they'd followed since Rick Chapman started at the Sales Center about five years earlier.

This home's open concept and wide plank floors would lend itself to amusements like family game nights or just thumbing through the channels on the huge flat screen TV hung above the stacked-stone fireplace. It was furnished with care.

The linen-covered sofas and a comfortable dining set in the eat-in kitchen were situated just so.

Bree's friend and fellow salesperson Jessie at the Sales Center had staged it just right, too. Bree breathed in the scent of fresh-baked cookies and let out a sigh. She wore her usual Monday morning attire, a linen skirt paired with a smooth-as-silk shirt. Today's top was sage green, and unbuttoned just enough in her opinion. A wide suede headband in the same color held her long hair back from her face and the sweet string of pearls around her neck matched the ones clinging to her earlobes.

The jewelry was a throwback from the country club days of her teen years, but wearing them made her feel a little bit closer to her grandmother. The sweet woman had passed away a year ago, and had in fact spurred Bree's pressing need for rebirth. She'd been in a holding pattern since getting out of college, and her grandmother's bequeath to Bree made it possible for her to live her own life. She was twenty-six years old, after all. It was time for her to be…something. She'd started at Cypress last spring, but maybe this spring would give her the magic reboot she was hoping for.

Sitting on over ten thousand sprawling acres, Cypress Corners encompassed some of the prettiest land in the region.

From the moment she'd toured the place over a year ago, she'd been a goner. It was a wild and beautiful place, and it grabbed a hold of her with its promise of rebirth.

It was unusual that more than half the land was set aside as a sanctuary for native plants and animals, and just maybe she would flourish here as well. The rest of the property was dedicated to expensive homes, retail stores, and award-winning recreational facilities. The picturesque town center and the many amenities made the sales aspect of her job a breeze, actually.

She'd used part of her inheritance to buy a house here for herself, choosing one in the more densely populated villages rather than splurging on one fronting the pristine lakeshore. Her home was a Craftsman-style also, though much smaller than this model. With three bedrooms including a large master, it suited her. Her home really lacked furniture, though. And that hominess Jessie and her husband Noah's home possessed. Bree was torn between heading up to Ikea or raiding her grandmother's storage unit that had also been bequeathed to her. She'd yet to make a decision either way.

As strange as it should be, this fake domesticity made her happy. She was marooned in this perfect house. Stationed in this perfect kitchen with sparkling quartz countertops and quirky yet unobtrusive decorations like small rustic milk pitchers and artfully-weathered tin canisters. Together it all presented a place where visitors felt welcomed and even seduced to stay a while.

There were days when she felt like she was part of the window-dressing too, but she'd always been viewed as the pretty prop. The perfect daughter. The perfect girlfriend. The perfect mess, actually. Her grandmother had been the only one who hadn't pushed her to be someone she wasn't.

She set the tray on the counter and slipped off the quilted oven mitt. This "living with the home" initiative was the brainchild of her boss, Rick Chapman. Actually, it was the developer's baby, and Mr. Forbes instilled respect and dedication that she couldn't ignore. She might be *just a salesgirl*, as her parents often said, but she was darn good at her job.

Running her hands over the crisp cobalt blue dish towel, she tweaked it until it hung perfectly over the wall oven's door handle. The alarm system chime dinged, signaling that the front door had been opened. Turning with a practiced smile, she faced the newcomer standing in the entry.

"Good morning, and welcome to the Spruce model," she said.

The tall, dark-haired man stopped short on the marble tiles, and from the raised eyebrows above his deep brown eyes she guessed he recognized her as much as she did him. His name was Derek something-or-other, and she remembered him as the guy from Chapman Financial who had come around on some clandestine assignment a year ago. He was as hot as she remembered, too.

Broad shoulders stretched the buff dress shirt that seemed to have been tailormade for him. A silk tie the color of chocolate led her eye to his narrow waist. He looked like something out of a preppy catalog spread set in the Hamptons, down to the scruff showing on his chiseled jaw.

The lack of a smile on his sculpted lips was familiar too. *Tall, dark and gloomy* was the nickname they'd all pinned on him then, and it seemed to still fit as well now as his pressed tan trousers did. The stormy weather outside seemed to fit his mood.

"Hello." He cleared his throat and ran a hand through his thick black waves. "I'm here to tour the model homes."

"I'm Bree James." She stepped closer, holding out her hand. "I'm the salesperson currently assigned to the green neighborhood of Cypress Corners."

"Derek Stone." He took her hand and gave it a firm shake. His voice was rumbly and warm, and quite unexpected given the cold rigidity stamped on his face. His patrician Boston accent was faint but there nonetheless. He continued to stare at her and goosebumps chased from their clasped hands up her arm. Her patrician-pale skin flushed and she guessed a blush now covered her face, too.

Withdrawing from his grasp, she folded her hands in front of her. "What can I do for you?"

He shrugged one shoulder. "Just give me the nickel tour."

She sensed something in his tone, a lack of enthusiasm that really ticked her off. "Look, if you're not interested I don't understand why you stopped by."

He blinked at her. "I'm interested. I want to know about the materials and structure too, not just see the layout and staged rooms."

Ah, here was that entitlement she had developed a distaste for in her own upbringing. She placed her hands on her hips. "Then why not just talk to Noah Brady? He's the builder here. Or maybe Ben Chapman?"

The guy nodded. "The architect, yeah. He's working on the Active Adult section too, isn't he?"

Bree's lips thinned. "That isn't for me to say. Why are you here again?"

He seemed to remember something and a smile flitted over his face. Wow, he was something else when he smiled. His eyes warmed and her flush deepened. Reflexively, she took another half-step back.

"Mr. Forbes sent me." He arched one dark brow. "I'm the new in-house counsel for Cypress Corners."

She gaped at him. "You're the new what now?"

"In-house counsel. You know, the attorney hired by Mr. Forbes to serve the development?"

"I thought they were bringing in an attorney from one of the big firms in Orlando."

He didn't seem put out by her statement, or the least bit worried either. "That isn't for me to say."

She shut her mouth with a snap. So he would throw her words back at her? He was a lawyer, after all. They traded in words, the more the better. That smile she'd glimpsed made a split-second reappearance and she sucked in a breath. Something about this guy just set off an alarm inside her. His dark, smoky eyes. His ridiculously-handsome face. His long, strong body.

"Let me show you around and then you can get back to the Sales Center."

Both brows rose now. "Trying to get rid of me?"

And now he was teasing her? She wanted a reboot, sure. A new life that was just her own. This guy was so not the new start she craved. He was your quintessential Type A, golf on Wednesdays, country club brunch on the weekends kind of guy. Been there, done that, finally off that hamster wheel.

A crack of thunder shook the windows as the skies opened up with a downpour. So much for a typical Monday morning.

Chapter 2

Derek drove his rented Lexus back to the Sales Center, his mind on the gorgeous girl who'd clearly been pissed at him. She'd been professional, of course. He wouldn't expect any less from one of Rick Chapman's people. She had seemed less than patient with him though, which didn't add up. He'd put on his usual professional persona, too.

He remembered her from last year's visit, though his mind had been cluttered then with way too much to think about flirting like Eli Graham had. He and Eli had scoped out the place and taken the required tours, but Eli was way more comfortable mixing in than Derek had ever been. The guy might have grown up in foster care, but at least he didn't have anybody to impress before he'd hooked up with Bill Chapman. As for Derek? He'd had to be on his guard almost from before he'd started prep school.

He parked his sleek sedan, the perfect car for his persona as a successful corporate lawyer and nearly identical to the lease he'd had back in Boston, in the crushed-shell lot adjacent to the Sales Center. The rain had let up but if the steel gray sky was any indication, more downpours would come over the course of the rest of the day.

The town center of Cypress Corners was quaint and welcoming. Though built less than fifteen years earlier it resembled any small town from up north. He should have felt at home here, since there was a real New England feel in the red brick and crisp white trim of the shops and other buildings. It was only his first day, and he really felt out of his element.

He'd foregone wearing a suit today, which was a first in his memory. Mr. Forbes had told him yesterday that they were a little more casual here in Cypress. Rick Chapman had been dressed much like Derek was, so that put him on a more even keel. The nautical terminology seemed to stick with him despite being out of that world for years.

He'd sailed in his youth, as the son of a prominent attorney in Boston might be expected to. Rowing crew at Boston College had filled his days between high school graduation and entering law school, and he still missed being around the water. He'd clerked for a law firm decidedly not his father's for a couple of years while studying for the bar, which hadn't given him much time for water sports.

Then he'd declined a partnership with the son-of-a-bitch to go and work for Bill Chapman in the heart of the city. Bill had worked him hard from the start, but since he worked just as hard as he'd expected Derek to, Derek had been only too glad to fall right into line.

Now, at twenty-eight, Derek didn't regret that decision in the least despite being all but banned from his family's yacht club. He knew just what came along with kowtowing to Edward Stone, esquire: indentured servitude and wading through a never-ending stream of bullshit to make Eddie look good.

Derek had read all of the stuff about the amenities in Cypress, and knew his love of the water could be easily indulged if he gave it a chance. There were even adventure courses, created and run by Jake Chapman, on the main lakeshore that might fill some of his time. Rick had told him this morning that Saturdays and Sundays the Sales Center and the model homes were closed. Mr. Forbes had said as much over the phone, but hearing it in person made it real.

As strange as that custom was, it seemed that Cypress Corners' bottom line was very healthy in spite of ignoring the lure of weekend home-shoppers. None of this should surprise him, though. Working with the tree-huggers, as Bill put it, was profitable as well as environmentally conscious. That shouldn't be true either, but it was.

The Cypress Institute, located across the street from the

Sales Center, was tasked with keeping the development firmly on the green side. It kept a careful eye toward the conservation of native plants and animals. Rick's wife Harmony was a plant conservationist and Ty Walsh, the guy married to his new boss's sister, looked after the animals. It really seemed like a family business, since so many of the key positions were held by Chapmans or Chapmans-by-marriage. Bill Chapman was right on one very big point. All of his kids came to Cypress and never came back.

Derek knew all of this, he was always one to do his due-diligence, but it would take some getting used to. That was for sure.

"Hey, Derek Stone!" a thin blond guy named Oliver called with a wave of a hand. "So you're back for your tour?"

"Hello, Oliver." Derek had met the guy before heading out to the green neighborhood that morning and joined him on the wide steps in front of the Sales Center. "I guess you're taking me around?"

Oliver gave a nod. "Sure am, Boston. I won the coin toss."

Derek couldn't tell if the guy was serious or teasing, but he found himself smiling. It seemed you couldn't help but smile when you were in this guy's company. Oliver was bright and shiny and seemed like he was always happy to be wherever he was.

"I thought Eli would be stuck with me," Derek said.

"Nope. Mr. Forbes and Eli have been in a meeting all morning."

Derek blinked. This had to be about the Active Adult community. He made a mental note to get with Eli later and pick his brain. Maybe he could talk him into having a beer at the Town Tavern after work.

Derek didn't just *want* to see his mother settled safely in Florida. No. He needed to see her out of Boston, out of Massachusetts, and far away from where his father could wield his usual brand of control over her. If she were in Florida with him, starting a new life and maybe making some new friends, he and Abby could breathe a little easier.

He opened one of the glass doors and waved Oliver in ahead of him. The older woman at the reception desk waved with a smile and Derek nodded in her direction.

"Good morning, Mrs. Walsh," Derek said to her.

"Did you enjoy your tour of the green neighborhood, dear?"

Derek brushed his damp hair back from his forehead. "I

did."

"Our Bree is a wonderful salesperson."

He stilled before slowly lowering his hand. "She is."

"And she's very easy on the eyes."

Derek's mouth dropped open. "She is," he said again.

"Mom, what are you doing?" Ty Walsh, Cassie Chapman's husband, smiled as he came into the lobby from the back hallway.

"Hello, son." Mrs. Walsh turned pink. "I'm not doing anything."

Ty smirked at her and shook his head. "Sorry about that, Derek. Sometimes my mother borrows more than a few pages from Lettie Fairfax's book."

Derek was at a loss now.

Ty chuckled and clasped Derek on the shoulder. "From that expression I guess you haven't met Lettie yet."

Derek thought for a second. "No, I don't think I have."

Oliver laughed out loud. "She's going to love you."

Derek looked over at Ty's mother, who was obviously trying to keep from grinning. "All right, then. I'll just go grab a bottle of water and Oliver and I can start the tour."

"And you're coming with me tomorrow." Ty ran an eye

over Derek's clothes, one brow arched. "And dress comfortably. We're doing the full-on eco tour on the east side of the property."

"Ah, the real tour I'll bet."

Ty blinked in an obvious show of innocence. "I took you on a real tour last year. You and Eli both."

"And Eli let me know that things are a little different once you've been shown the secret handshake."

That made Ty smile. Derek headed toward the breakroom to grab his water. He suspected they would talk about him once he left the reception area, but since they'd already talked about him to his face he wasn't too put out by it. He'd bought into the whole thing once he'd spoken with Rick this morning. He was fully on-board, and he should try to fit in.

The hard part would be joining the crowd without letting them get to know the real him. He knew from past experience that it would be a real disappointment.

***

"So how did this morning go?"

Bree looked up from her yogurt cup to nod to Jessie Brady. The breakroom in the Sales Center, a space with a couple of round tables and a kitchenette, was empty except for the two of them. Her friend wore her usual cardigan, but today's was spring green to fit her sunny Pixie personality.

"The usual Monday, Jessie. How about yours?"

Jessie smirked and sat down across from her. "You were living with the house, Bree. Was it as stifling as I'm afraid it is?"

Bree shrugged. "It's weird, but it's kind of comfortable. Part of the credit goes to your staging. The house really feels like a home."

Jessie waved away the compliment, much like she usually did. "You baked the cookies."

Now Bree laughed. "Okay, you've got me. Ate a couple of them, too."

"What about tall, dark and gloomy?"

"Who?" Like she didn't know.

Jessie snorted. "Come on, Bree. Boston?"

Bree blinked, but managed to keep her expression even. "He came for a quick tour."

"And now he's out with Ollie."

"Oh?" She didn't care about Derek Stone's whereabouts. Nope.

"Noah says he'll be good for Cypress but I'm not so sure."

Jessie's husband, Noah Brady, was the builder in the green

neighborhood and the upcoming Active Adult village. He was a good guy, a great father and a wonderful husband. Bree figured he was a good judge of character, too.

"What's bothering you about him, Jessie?"

"I don't know exactly. It's just that last year, when he came here with Eli? They were clearly on some sort of fishing expedition for Chapman Financial."

Bree had gotten the same vibe from the two of them but after getting to know Eli better since, and seeing how over-the-moon he was for his pregnant wife Caro, she was less inclined to accept the secret spy theory they'd all talked about a year ago. Derek Stone didn't seem to be anything more than as he appeared. He looked every inch the privileged prep-school lawyer he was.

"But now Derek is working for Rick and Mr. Forbes," Bree pointed out. "Both of them have said again and again that having an in-house counsel would be beneficial to Cypress."

"But what if he's still working for Bill Chapman?"

"He is," Rick Chapman said, coming into the breakroom.

Bree looked at her boss. "He is?"

"My father was clear on this, actually," Rick said. "Except where there might be a conflict of interest, Derek remains on retainer with Chapman."

Jessie looked surprised but Bree wasn't. If Mr. Forbes wanted the guy, he had to be a valuable asset. That value had to extend all the way back up to Chapman Financial.

Bree had met Bill Chapman when Jake and Claire's baby was born last fall. He was a big guy, tall and broad like his sons, and possessed a commanding personality. If anyone other than Arthur James had raised Bree, she might have been intimidated. As it was, she merely pitied all of the Chapman kids for having the blustering man as their father.

They'd all seemed to have carved out lives of their own, and appeared very happy with their work, love and life choices. When looked at in that light, the Chapmans gave Bree the hope that she could find herself here in Cypress too.

"...sitting down with Derek sometime this week, Bree," Rick said.

"Hmm?" Bree looked at her boss again. "I'm sorry, what did you say?"

Rick gave her a small smile. "I would like everyone to sit down sometime this week with Derek and help bring him up to speed."

"What could we possibly tell him?" Jessie asked, stating

the question Bree was about to ask.

"He'll be in just about everything that happens at the Sales Center, Jessie," Rick said. "Reviewing contracts, lease agreements, residents' disputes, among other things." Rick smiled a little bit wider. "I'm sure Mr. Forbes will call a meeting about it tomorrow."

They all shared a knowing nod. Mr. Forbes did love his meetings. Rick left the breakroom and Jessie whistled.

"So bringing Boston into the fold really *was* necessary," Jessie said. "Or someone like him, anyway."

"Rick's right. Having an in-house counsel is probably long overdue."

"He's going to be handling a lot of crud, too. Things like paint colors and fences, and other resident complaints and applications."

"Ugh, what does Noah say about that?"

Jessie grinned. "Noah really can't stand the guy currently in charge of design reviews. Calls him a blowhard, among other things."

"Yikes," Bree said. "I almost feel sorry for Derek."

"Why?" Derek asked.

Bree jumped in her seat, sending her spoon clattering to the tabletop. He stood in the doorway, his brows drawn together over his eyes. He looked perplexed. It was the most emotion she'd ever glimpsed on his face, actually.

"I just meant..." she began.

Jessie rushed to her feet. "Well, I have a tour in ten minutes."

The Pixie flew out of the breakroom, leaving Bree alone with Derek. It was obviously raining again, because drops sparkled in his dark waves. His pressed shirt looked a little less starchy now, from flecks of water and the wild way she knew Ollie liked to drive the golf carts on his tours.

He crossed the room to the coffee maker and proceeded to make himself a cup. He appeared very capable, and she had to admit that his tailored pants clung nicely to his firm butt. She shouldn't be noticing things like that about this guy, but there it was. Hello!

"Now why do you feel sorry for me?" he asked as he turned back to her.

She blinked at the intensity in his gaze. "I just meant that you're going to be dealing with a very different world than the one you left in Boston."

"How do you know what I left in Boston?"

"I don't, exactly. But Cypress is unique. And special."

He tilted his head to one side, his gaze sharpening. "You like it here."

"Of course I do," she said. "I wouldn't live here if I didn't love it."

"But, you work here too."

"Yes. Is that so strange?"

He seemed to want to ask her something but the hiss of the coffee maker drew his attention. As he turned away from her again, she wondered about their odd aborted conversation. He'd come to work here, of course. He might end up living here or he might not. It wasn't a requirement of employment at Cypress Corners, though she'd yet to meet anyone who came here to work and didn't buy into the whole package.

Maybe he would commute from Orlando. That wasn't unheard of, not that she would ever want to go back to that world. She hadn't grown up in Orlando proper but in an elite area northeast of the city in Heathrow. No matter what he chose to do, it wasn't her concern.

Her attention strayed to him as he faced her again. Those capable-looking hands gripped that coffee mug. That long, lean body leaned easily against the counter at his back. She could smell him, too. Like crisp spring rain and something else a little spicy. She nodded at whatever he said, her eyes on his sculpted lips.

"Great. Just let me know when," he said.

"When?"

"When you're free." He shrugged one broad shoulder. "To show me some available properties?"

She squared her shoulders and refocused. "Just text me what you're looking for and I'll get a list together."

He nodded and walked toward the doorway. "We'll grab a bite to eat afterwards."

"Um, okay. Sure."

He looked as puzzled as she was by his invitation, but then he was gone. She sat back. She was spending more time with him. Great. They were going to eat dinner or something, too. She should push him off onto Jessie. That woman seemed immune to Derek's charms. Bree? Not so much. Hadn't she agreed to something while staring at him like some lovesick teenager?

She was a professional. She knew Cypress inside and out. She would find him a place to live, hopefully in one of the more exclusive villages because why not go for a larger commission?

And then she would keep her distance. How hard could it

be?

Chapter 3

Derek sat in the courtyard of the coffee shop Wednesday afternoon, sipping his coffee as he thumbed through the listings Bree had sent him this morning. He was staying at the Cypress Inn and, although it was comfortable and surprisingly luxurious, he didn't want to stay there indefinitely. It was fashioned like a grand Victorian manor, and that décor and theme carried through until you climbed up to the guest rooms. There you might be in any high-end hotel room, given the furnishings and ambiance. Still, it would never feel like home.

He had to pick a place that didn't only suit him. His mother would need somewhere to stay until her own home was ready. From what he'd learned from Eli and Noah, it could be months before the first residents could move into the new section. Abby was on Mom-watch for now, but she was busy trying to make a place for herself in the competitive veterinarian business. Damn, but he'd like to see her move down here too.

Bree hadn't seemed like she wanted to help him but she was the one Mr. Forbes had recommended. After their short conversation in the breakroom it was clear that he'd obviously surprised her when he'd asked her to grab dinner with him afterwards. He'd surprised himself too.

She was easy on the eyes, of course. Even in those conservative clothes she wore, her curves rocked a look just this side of sexy. He hadn't missed the number of buttons undone, letting the V of her soft-looking shirt give him just a peek at what he guessed were some stellar tits.

She was taller than the Pixie girl, the one married to Noah Brady. Not quite as tall as Ben Chapman's wife, though. He would bet that if he were to stand really close to Bree, toe to toe, she would fit nicely against him. Especially if he grabbed her beneath her round little ass and pulled her up onto her toes.

He gave himself a mental shake. Clicking a few of the choices to select, he sent them back to Bree. He wasn't in Cypress looking to hook up, especially with a woman like her. He knew the type. Hell, he'd gotten involved with the type while traveling in those country-club circles. They were usually pretty staid and cold until you took them to bed a couple of times. Then they started wrangling for a ring.

His last entanglement had gone so far as to approach his father to get his help dragging Derek to the altar. If she'd looked past her surgery-perfect nose she would have seen that he had no relationship with his father, let alone any respect for the asshole's opinion.

Mostly, he'd never dated much once he'd started at Chapman. Just a few casual drinks that led to a few casual nights. He sure as hell wasn't going to date someone he worked with, not even someone as tempting as Bree. He'd rather get his rocks off with some nameless pickup at one of the bars over in St. Cloud than risk involving anyone at Cypress in his relationship drama.

"Hey, Derek."

He looked up to see Eli walking toward him. "Hey, Eli. What's up?"

"Just grabbing a drink and a treat from the bakery."

Eli lifted his chin toward Sweet Escape, the bakery Derek knew his wife owned. The bright green paper bag he held was giving off the scent of lemon and something else Derek couldn't identify.

"What's in there?" he asked.

Eli winked. "Something Caro is trying out. Lemon lavender scones."

Derek's mouth watered. "Can I try one?"

Eli shook his head. "Nope. I'm her official Guinea pig."

"Selfish bastard."

"Such is my curse," Eli teased. "She's getting to where she

doesn't trust her sense of taste. Pregnant taste buds, or something like that."

Eli's wife was expecting, but Derek didn't know more than that.

"How far along is she?"

Eli beamed a smile. "Just about half way."

Derek nodded absently. It seemed like there were babies everywhere. He'd seen Ben and Tammy Chapman pushing a stroller just this morning. Jake Chapman had paraded around his and Claire's little redheaded cherub yesterday at the close of business. Derek supposed they were cute, the babies. But he had little experience with kids and didn't really miss it. Abby was three years younger than he was, so he couldn't really remember her as an infant except in pictures. Maybe when Abby settled down Derek would rouse enthusiasm for being a doting uncle.

"Family looks good on you," he said to Eli.

Eli visibly sobered as a seldom-seen serious expression crossed his face. "Thanks, man. You don't know how good it feels. Believe me."

Derek knew how hard it had been on Eli, bouncing around foster care since he was a little kid. He'd made that disclosure one night after a long day, but Derek hadn't given up anything about his own family in return. His stomach clenched and his eyes pricked. Clearing his throat, he straightened.

"I wanted to talk to you more about the Active Adult property, Eli."

Eli's brows rose but he gave a slow nod. "About time you came clean."

Derek laughed a little. "Hey, we talked a little bit about it yesterday."

"Yeah, but you're forgetting one thing. I was on that little reconnaissance mission with you last year."

"Now I couldn't care less about the impact of the development on Chapman. I'm solely interested as a potential buyer."

"You? Ah." Eli gave a sage nod. "Your mother."

Derek's face grew a little hot but he fought through his embarrassment. "I know I haven't told you much, but she needs her own place. A new start, really. In a new place."

Eli threw his arms out wide, his expression bright again. "Buddy, there's no new place better than Cypress."

"Here, here," a musical voice intoned from a table just across the courtyard. Derek noticed an older woman seated beneath a tree dotted with pink flowers. She held up a glass in their direction. "I couldn't say it better myself."

"See?" Eli grinned. "Lettie agrees with me."

So this was Lettie. Derek wasn't sure how he'd missed her. She wore a bright yellow smock, green crocs and a big straw hat. Her smile was a bit sly and her eyes sparkled.

"And on that note, I'll leave you to your interrogation." Eli came to his feet and bowed in Lettie's direction. "Ma'am."

"Oh, go on with you," the woman said with a grin.

Derek watched Eli walk towards the Sales Center and then came to his feet. He crossed the short distance to her table.

"Derek Stone, ma'am," he said with a sharp nod. "It's a pleasure to meet you."

The woman's blue eyes, peeking from beneath a fringe of silvery hair, sparkled. "Charlotte Fairfax, Derek Stone. Please, call me Lettie. You have even more of that Boston crispness than our Eli."

"Eli has lived down here for some time." Derek shrugged. "I think that would change a man."

"On the surface, perhaps." Lettie pushed away her glass of iced tea and folded her hands on top of what looked like flower catalogues. "It has been my experience that a person doesn't change who he is at his core."

"You might be right on that count."

"Our Elijah, however? This life, the love and family he's found here, might not be what he was born into but I suspect it fits him better than whatever it is he left behind in Boston."

"I concede the point on that as well, Lettie."

Her eyes narrowed. "What did you leave behind, dear Derek?"

His spine stiffened. This woman might ooze Southern charm, but she wasn't going to get him to spill anything about his life.

"I left a job at Chapman Financial," he gave in lame answer.

She gave a nod. "I believe there might be more to you than you appear." She winked. "Not that you don't present a fine specimen."

He found a smile. "It was a pleasure meeting you, Lettie. But I have an appointment I have to keep."

"With our dear Sabrina, yes."

Sabrina? Bree. "Yes."

"Go then, Derek Stone. Don't keep her waiting."

He bowed his head to her as Eli had, it seemed to be the proper thing to do anyway, and followed his friend's lead to the

Sales Center.

Lettie's words still rattled around in his head, though. Eli definitely had a different life from the one he'd had in Boston. Was that really a possibility for him?

Shoving that thought aside, he focused on finding a place to start his new life. He'd worry about actually living it later.

***

Bree clicked closed the docs on her laptop and began shutting things down. It was nearly four o'clock but Rick had told her to take off a little bit early today since she was technically still working while showing Derek some properties. It had been Jessie's turn in the model home, after Bree had sat there until lunch time. Bree had gone through the houses Derek had selected from the list she'd sent him and was ready to give him a different kind of tour.

"Off to show Boston some hot properties?" Ollie grinned as he settled his hip on the corner of her desk. "Or just some properties to hot Boston?"

Bree just shook her head at him. Except for Tammy and Eli, the sales people all shared a large workspace. Her desk wasn't far from Ollie's, or Jessie's for that matter. There were no half-walls or cubicles, thank God. Just an open space where they could work when they weren't out touring prospective homeowners or marooned in one of the models. The result was a comradery she hadn't expected. She should have, though. Rick Chapman never did anything by accident.

"It's just a house tour, Ollie. Nothing to get your panties in a twist over."

Ollie chuckled. "Then it's a good thing I'm not wearing any."

Bree laughed. "TMI, brother."

Ollie waved a hand. "Kidding. Ask Tammy. I only wear boxer briefs."

"Don't drag me into this." Tammy Chapman joined them, giving Oliver a playful shove. "And don't pretend you keep me in the loop on your underwear choices."

Bree shoved her laptop in her bag and tucked her phone in her purse. "I'll leave you two to your quarrel, then. I have houses to show."

Tammy placed a hand on Bree's arm. "Don't sweat it, Bree. Derek might have a big stick up his ass, but from what I remember about our illustrious boss Rick? He had one when he first came down here too."

"Never mind," Rick said from the hallway.

Tammy laughed and flicked her long dark hair back over one shoulder. "Tell me you were easygoing back then, Rick."

Rick smiled at his sister-in-law but Ollie wore a comical look of fear.

Bree shook her head. "I'm not sweating anything. I showed Derek what I have and he told me what he likes." She winced. "I know what that sounds like, Ollie."

Tammy snorted. "Have a good tour, Bree."

Bree nodded and headed out toward the lobby. She shouldn't have been surprised, but she found him waiting for her when she approached the reception desk.

"Are you ready to go?" he asked in that clipped voice.

"All set." She sounded a little bit nervous to herself, despite what she'd told Tammy and Oliver. "Let's do this."

His lips curved upward in one corner but he waved towards the front doors. "After you."

They climbed into one of the charged and ready golf carts. She'd chosen a four-seater, since one of the other salespeople might get a larger group to tour sometime this afternoon and need one of the six-seaters. Derek slid his big body into the passenger seat as Bree stowed her bags behind the driver's.

The golf cart was outfitted for touring guests, prospective

residents and investors. It had comfortable leather seats, a jaunty green, white and burgundy striped awning, and big fat tires that made the ride smooth.

He took up more than the space allowed for a passenger, and draped his arm over the back of her seat. His fresh, spicy scent wrapped around her and she indulged in a deep breath.

"Onward, Sabrina," he said.

"Bree," she said quickly. "Only my mother and father call me Sabrina."

He held up a hand. "Sorry. Lettie called you that today."

She pulled away from the curb and steered towards the main lakeshore. "You met Lettie today, did you?"

He chuckled, but the rasping laugh seemed unusual for him. "Sure did. I guess I passed muster."

"Passed muster? Hmm. I'll just bet she put you through your paces."

"She's something, all right."

He fell silent and she wondered just what their resident relationship sorceress thought of his fine self. She looked at him from the corner of her eye as they took a right turn. He'd ditched the tie she'd seen on him earlier, and his slate gray shirt had two buttons undone. He appeared a little more relaxed than she'd seen him previously, too. It could be the wind blowing his thick waves around, though.

"I thought you'd like to live near the lakeshore," she said after they'd ridden for a while. "Do you like the setting of the inn?"

"Yes, I do. I believe Rick and Harmony Chapman live over in that village."

She nodded. "Few homes come available there, but I sent you what I've found. There are more of the smaller homes available, which you saw from my list. Some of them are quite nice."

He nodded and brushed his hair back from his forehead. "I defer to your judgment, Bree."

"Then let's start big and work our way down."

She took his silence as agreement and they were soon parked in front of a home set on a corner with a wide wraparound porch that would afford a beautiful view of the main lakeshore. It was traditional in style but she knew that, like the other homes in Cypress, it was state-of-the-art at its guts. Residents were connected both through wire and wirelessly to communication, security and entertainment, and even in these homes outside the green neighborhood there was a healthy dose of environmentally-responsible materials used throughout.

Switching off the motor, she faced him. "What do you think?"

The expression on his face was inscrutable. She could see him taking in every inch of the house's façade, and when he gave a small nod she supposed he liked it. What was there not to like? She knew from Jessie that the house had been empty for two months now, and that the current homeowner lived up in North Carolina.

"This is for rent or for sale?" He stepped out and stared up at the house. "Do you have that info?"

She swallowed down the sharp retort on her tongue and nodded. "The homeowner priced it for sale but will consider a rental." She passed him and stepped up onto the vacant porch. As she unlocked the coded key box, she caught him staring across the street.

"You could fit several chairs out here," she said. "Maybe a porch swing. This is northwest-facing, so you'll have cross breezes throughout the day and a good view of the sunset."

"It's a nice view."

Wow. That was an understatement. Their footsteps echoed through the house as they walked from one room to the next. It was a gorgeous home, with dark wood planking on the floors and a spacious open-concept living and kitchen area.

"One of these front rooms would make a great office. There's also a guest room with full bath toward the back of the house that serves as a changing room should you put in a pool."

Derek was quiet as she led him through a tour of the lovely home. She pointed out the bedrooms with their shared bathroom as well as the oversized master bedroom with attached bathroom which rivaled any you might find in a top-tier hotel. Aside from a few sounds of agreement, grunts really, he simply followed her through the second floor and nodded as she illustrated the home's features.

They arrived where they'd started after just ten minutes. Derek stopped in the kitchen, one hand on the sparkling gray quartz countertop. Once again, he wore that shuttered expression. As he fisted one hand at his side, she found herself reaching out to touch his arm.

"Derek?"

He faced her, his dark eyes stormy. "Do what you have to. I'll take it. Purchase, not rent."

Her mouth dropped open. "What?" She had to have heard him incorrectly. "You want this house? But we haven't even looked at the others."

"This one will do. It's big enough and I like where it is."

Bree's mind worked. The house was priced well, but his quick decision seemed out of character with what she knew about his reputation for being meticulous.

"Are you sure?"

His eyes flashed at her. "Are you questioning me?"

She blew out a breath. "Hey, it's not my place to question you. But why don't you want to see the other houses?"

His jaw visibly tightened. "I'm not going to explain what it is. The place is right. That's all."

Recognition dawned on her. "You mean it feels right?"

His gaze slid away from hers. "Maybe."

"Like home? I know it looks a lot like a New England Colonial. Is it like the home where you grew up?"

"It's nothing like where I grew up," he bit out.

She blinked and he cursed softly. "I'm sorry," he said. "The house does remind me of New England. I think…I like it because of that. It will be a comfortable transition."

"A transition?" Now she was completely confused. "Derek, what are you talking about?"

He swallowed audibly, his eyes shiny now. "I'm sorry. I

didn't mean to lose it, especially in front of someone like you."

"Someone like me?" Oh, he was such an irritating guy. "What is that supposed to mean?"

He ran his eyes over her. That chill was back again. "Privileged. Spoiled."

Echoes of what she'd been pegged as for her whole life crashed through her. "Excuse me?" She fisted her hands at her sides. "You don't even know me."

"I know women like you." His eyes raked over the front of her. "Hell, I've *had* women like you. You judge things, you judge people, by what they can give you. That's their worth to you."

Anger flared and before she could stop herself she raised her hand and slapped him across the face. Hard.

"Don't you dare talk to me that way!"

He touched his cheek, his eyes closed tight. He murmured something she couldn't catch before facing her again. "I'm sorry."

Something in the tone of his voice, in the hurt she now saw in his eyes, drew her closer to him. Her anger left as quickly as it had come. "Derek?"

He wrapped her in his arms, his hold so tight she could

hardly breathe. "I'm sorry, Bree." He buried his face in the crook of her neck. "I'm so sorry."

He pulled back and she looked up at him. She knew what was coming. Her pulse tripped and her breath quickened. *Oh, my.*

And then he kissed her.

Chapter 4

Derek couldn't think of anything but holding this girl in his arms. He'd been a dick. He knew that. He'd all but called her a grasping bitch and she'd had every right to slap him. Kissing her, though? That was something Derek hadn't imagined he could crave so much.

Her lips were soft. Warm. Her body fit against his just as he'd imagined. Her tongue was quick on his as he tasted her even more deeply. Pulling back slightly, he nuzzled the sweet-smelling skin at the side of her neck.

"Bree." He breathed her in, the scent of spring flowers and a hint of sugar. "Damn, Bree."

She made some kind of soft sound and pressed against him. His hands cupped her ass and lifted her against him, grinding as he let desire rule him. Just for a second. Just enough to tease her with how amazing they could be together. He didn't deserve it, though. No matter how good she felt, she tasted, he couldn't put his own brand of shit on her.

For a split-second his heated brain worked around the wisdom of getting her naked right now. In this house that would in all probability be his soon. God, he wanted her. His arms tightened and she trembled. As his hands lifted her skirt, his fingers stroking over the backs of her toned thighs, he felt her change. Stiffen. He released her as he sought to collect himself.

She took advantage of his loosened hold and stepped back out of his arms. "Whoa," she breathed.

He instinctively made a move to follow her but she pressed a hand against his chest. "Hold it," she said.

She closed her eyes and took in a breath, but he saw that her hand trembled as she smoothed her hair back down. He hadn't even been aware of it but he must have run his fingers through all that golden silk. His pulse was pounding and his dick was hard. He had to rein this in and fast.

"Bree, look."

She opened those gorgeous blue eyes and stared up at him. "What was that?"

He was damned if he knew. "It was just a kiss."

He was lying. He knew it and she knew it, but he would hold to his story. It was the single best few seconds he'd spent in at least three years, but how could he tell her that? She would never believe it. He'd sound like an idiot at best and an asshole at worst.

Her lips parted, those soft wet lips of hers, and she shook her head. "Whatever. That is so not going to happen again."

He licked his own lips and could still taste her. His mouth, his body, might still crave something more but his head knew what was what. "You're right."

She straightened her skirt and visibly collected herself. A lot more buttons of her shirt were undone than previously, and he caught a glimpse of those fantastic breasts not quite covered by pink lace. His mouth watered but he managed to merely point toward her cleavage. "Your shirt."

She looked down and her eyes widened. She gasped and fumbled a little as she did up the buttons. "Jeez."

"Sorry."

"Stop apologizing, Derek."

He recalled then that he'd said he was sorry over and over again as he'd kissed and caressed her. He bit back another apology. God, old habits die hard.

"This never happened," she added.

That pissed him off a little bit. It was the single best kiss he'd had in as long as he could remember, but he knew it meant nothing. He'd been a dick and she'd been right to slap him. It was the first time in his memory that he'd deserved it, despite the many reasons his father had always given. He hadn't been right to kiss her, though. He nodded his agreement.

"So let me know the details of the offer," he said. "I think we can come in near asking."

"You really want this house."

"I do."

She stared at him for a beat. He fought to push back the echoes of desire still thrumming through him, keeping his expression even.

"Okay, then," she said.

They left the home and all the way back to the Sales Center he couldn't shake the memory of what had happened in that kitchen. His hands itched to run all over her body, and without the barrier of her very nice, very professional clothes. He'd told her he'd had women like her? He was out of his mind if he believed he had ever been with a woman like Bree.

From the first time he'd met her he'd been blunt. Remote, as he sought to be in all business interactions. All through the tour of the house he'd been preoccupied though. This choice was important. He had to find a place where his mother would be comfortable as she transitioned into a normal life. He wanted that for her more than anything in this world. His job, his money, his car. All of it paled as he thought about everything his mother had endured with Eddie Stone.

He and Abby had felt the brunt of their father's anger or inadequacies now and then. Over and over Derek would apologize but it never seemed to be good enough. Their mother had taken everything the bastard had given her without protest, though. Barely a year had passed since Derek and Abby's repeated arguments finally led to a long-overdue divorce.

"I'll be in touch," Bree said as she cranked off the golf cart's motor.

As she made a move to step out, he placed a hand on her arm. "Bree, wait."

She turned to him, her cheeks flushed and her hair a little mussed from the ride. His mind flashed back to how she'd looked after their kiss. How she would have looked afterwards if he'd gotten her up on that sparkly quartz countertop.

"What is it?" she asked. "Don't even think we're going to do dinner. Not now."

Her tone was ice cold and just what he needed to douse his adolescent fantasies.

"I *am* sorry."

She arched one perfectly-shaped brow. "I believe you."

He dipped his head. "And I know you told me to let this go, and I will. I just wanted you to know that."

"I want you to forget this ever happened."

"I will."

Her gaze ran over his face before she gave a nod. Stepping out, giving him a nice shot of her even nicer legs, she left him alone in the cart.

He took the time to breathe slowly, in and out. He'd had to figure out a way to handle his own anger at his father growing up. He'd had to swallow every hurtful word and painful blow the bastard had flung at him. Hell, he'd had to watch his father hit his mother until he was big enough to stand in front of her for protection. He'd be damned if he forgot the reason he was doing this.

Moving here. Starting over. He was doing it for his family. The family that counted. For his mother and for his sister. Of that, he was very sure. He was sure of something else, too.

There was no way in hell he would ever forget about kissing Bree.

***

Bree sat on her porch that evening, sipping a glass of wine as she waited for the sun to dip behind the trees. A creamy chenille blanket wrapped her shoulders and her feet were tucked under her. It was a little bit chilly and more than a little bit damp,

57

but the sky was clear and pretty. She took another sip of the very nice pinot and let out a breath.

Her work day wasn't a long one, and she was generally free by five thirty at the latest. Today had been even shorter for her, since Derek had made his snap judgment about the very first house she'd shown him. She shook her head. Nope. She wasn't going to think about that confusing man. Not while she had her own slice of paradise here on her porch with nothing across the street but the tree-lined walk around the west side of the main lakeshore.

She knew the value of her own house. The neighborhood might not be as exclusive as her boss's or even Derek's but her home was situated on an exterior lot which gave her the feeling of space. She could enjoy it, and did. Often.

Most of her colleagues were on the same work schedule, but they all had their own lives. Tammy and Ben went home to their little ravioli Raffaella. Claire went home to her husband and their baby boy. Jessie and Noah had shared custody of Noah's son Max, and even Oliver had his significant other, Todd. But Bree didn't share her view or her more-than-adequate situation. Bree had no one. So she'd grabbed a yoga class at the fitness center and then come home. Alone.

Her house was lovely, but it was about time she did something about decorating it. This teak bench was pretty nice, and she'd gone to the home improvement center in St. Cloud to buy it and its comfy cushions. Taking a page from Jessie's book, she knew that the little things could improve a house's curb appeal. She might not be selling her place, but she sure liked coming home to its welcoming covered front porch.

The bench with bright pillows, the spring-greenery wreath hung on the glossy yellow door that perfectly accented the gray clapboard-look siding. It was kind of like sitting in one of those Easter eggs with the scene hidden inside. Once she walked through the front door, though? Any comfort or hominess was decidedly missing on the interior.

She should finally pay a visit to her grandmother's storage unit. Maybe over this weekend. It would give her something to do with her days off, anyway. Spending another weekend sitting on her very nice linen couch while watching movies back-to-back on her flat screen TV was really getting old. What would be on but romantic comedies or mistress-revenge movies anyway? Neither appealed. Romance, either quirky and sweet or dark and disturbed, wasn't on her horizon. She smiled at that last bit, grateful that without the highs of romance in her life she'd also never experienced the lows.

In truth, any kind of romance had always eluded her. The boys her parents had tried to throw in her path hadn't even spiked her pulse for one second. Then, when she was in college, the guys who just wanted to get in the ice-queen's pants weren't the kind a girl pinned her heart on, either. So she'd never even really dated. Once in a while a friend or coworker would set her up on a blind date, and she would indulge in the wish that she'd feel something for once.

There had been some mutual itch-scratching, of course. Some more-or-less-than-passionate hookups that always seemed to convince her that there would be no repeat. The guys always wanted more, but they were obviously thinking on a baser level. She liked sex. It was a way to fill a night once in a very great while. But it always left her a little cold. Maybe even as cold as some guys had always said she was.

Running the tip of her tongue over her upper lip, she indulged in reliving today's kiss. With Derek Stone, of all men. His touch, his taste, left her anything but cold. She'd felt herself come alive for those few moments in his arms. His hands on her butt, his hair-roughened face against her throat. How she'd had the strength to push him away, she had no idea. She'd wanted more of him, but that was ridiculous. She'd slapped the sneer off of his face and then kissed him like her plane was going down.

"Stupid mistake," she murmured. "Nothing more."

Oh, but that mistake was such a contradiction. He'd looked so lost, standing in that magnificent kitchen. Then she'd gone and pushed into his business and the stick-up-his-butt version she'd come to know had swiftly resurfaced. He'd looked at her and spoken to her like those guys at school had. And she'd slapped him! Jeez, what a mess.

There would be no repeat, though. She'd made that clear to him and he'd seemed on board with the plan. Heck, he'd seemed like he would barely remember their kiss past the short ride back to the Sales Center. It was a little insulting, really. She only had to close her eyes and she was back in that state-of-the-art kitchen. Back in his arms and under his spell.

She laughed lightly and drained her glass. Holding her breath, she watched as the sun slid below the ripples of the lake. The sky was orange and pink and purple.

"Hey, Bree," Derek said, poised on the sidewalk.

She'd been so focused on the view that she'd missed the sound of footsteps. He'd apparently walked here, since she didn't see his Lexus at the curb. He'd changed into jeans and sneakers, and she was a little surprised that he had either in his possession. His shirt was denim too, in a shade a little lighter than his pants.

"Hey." *Ugh, lame.*

He stuck his hands in his front pockets and stared down at his feet. She took the opportunity to really look at him. His forearms were corded with muscles she'd felt earlier today, but his sleeves were pushed up to showcase them. He looked different, he looked casual, and that served to put her on her guard.

"How did you find my house?"

He stared at her for a beat. "Due diligence."

"What do you want, Derek?"

His lips thinned, but he shrugged. "I have to talk to you about what happened today."

"Nothing happened today." She looked him dead in the eye. "Remember?"

"Bree, I was a dick."

"Okay, I'm listening."

He barked a short laugh and stepped closer. "May I?"

It was ridiculous, his standing on her front walkway and asking permission to approach. Surreal, even.

"Look, if you're going to apologize again I don't want to hear it."

"I don't have an apology. Just an explanation."

She stood. "I'll be right back."

"Where are you going?"

"I have the feeling this is going to call for wine. Am I wrong?"

A smile teased his mouth and his shoulders seemed to relax a little. "No. You're not wrong."

She gave a nod and went into the house to grab the bottle and another glass. When she returned to the porch he was still standing, but leaning a shoulder against one of the turned posts.

"Sit, Derek."

He nodded and sat on her comfy bench, placing his hands on his thighs. "Thanks."

She poured him a glass and handed it to him. He held it with long graceful fingers. She was surprised to see that small scars were visible on his palm. It was strange to think of him as a man with any flaws.

"Spill," she said.

"I need the house right away, Bree. For my mother."

She blinked. "Your mother? She's moving to Cypress?"

"That's the plan. I want her settled in the Active Adult section, but I don't want to wait until the development is ready for its first occupants."

She nodded. "That could be a while, actually."

"Right. I need you to keep this quiet, though."

"Oh, I don't know about that. I'm not much of a secret-keeper and I never lie."

"I'm not asking you to lie. I just need some discretion."

"Discretion? Yes, I'm used to that. I handle a lot of contracts."

He flashed that small smile again. "Contracts I suspect I'll be drafting going forward."

She smiled in return. "Then you have my word, counselor."

After drinking some of his wine, he set the glass on the porch floor. "I'll leave you alone, then."

He looked so lost, and she knew he had no real friends in Cypress but Eli. Eli and Caro would be spending their time together, though. She herself knew what it felt like to be the third wheel, and wouldn't want to wish it on the guy.

"What are you doing this weekend?" she asked.

"Nothing. Why?"

"Want to come up to Orlando with me? I have to go to my grandmother's storage unit."

"Okay."

"We'll need to borrow a truck, though. I've seen that car of yours and it just won't do."

"And what do you drive?"

"My grandmother's sixty-five Mustang. A sixty-five and a half, actually."

His mouth dropped open. "That's yours? I've seen it in the parking lot. Nice ride. And it was your grandmother's?"

She grinned as she thought of her inherited, cherry-red beauty. "My grandmother was one of a kind and my grandfather indulged her. They were a perfect match, and that car was one of her prized possessions."

"And now it's yours."

"Yep. And so is the contents of her storage unit. I'm going to warn you, though. I don't even know what's in there."

"Challenge accepted. I'll ask around and get a truck we can use."

"Thanks."

He stood and gave a nod. "Just let me know what time, Bree."

She nodded too, keeping to her seat. If she stood she'd probably throw herself at him and that so wasn't going to happen. This casual Derek was even more irresistible than the pressed and polished guy who she could still taste even over her wine.

He walked back towards the inn and she couldn't help but watch him go. Why had she asked him to go with her to Orlando? Because she was getting a little tired of being alone. Of living in the limbo she'd inhabited for the past year.

Or maybe she was afraid of missing out on what might be a pretty great second kiss.

Chapter 5

"Thanks, man." Derek took the keys from Eli. They stood on the front porch of Eli and Caro's townhouse, and the morning was a little chilly. It would get warmer later, but for now he slid the keys into the pocket of his hooded jacket. "I'll get these back to you this afternoon."

Eli waved a hand. "No hurry." He jerked a thumb toward the front door at his back. "I don't plan on driving anywhere this weekend, let alone dragging my wife out of bed to do it."

Derek arched a brow. "Laying it on a little thick, aren't you?"

Eli shook his head and grinned. "Nope. My cupcake gets up at oh dark thirty to open her bakery every day but Sunday. From this afternoon until the wee hours on Monday morning she's all mine. Her and that little bun she's got in her oven."

Derek chuckled at the guy's joke. "Bun. I get it. Okay, thanks again."

"No prob."

Derek left his Lexus parked in front of the townhouse and climbed into Eli's truck. The vehicle was big and beefy, and not what he would have expected his friend to own. An upscale SUV, maybe. Then again, there was a lot of country-feel to living in Cypress Corners. Maybe it made sense to have a sturdy truck that could haul stuff, too. Eli would have to pick up baby furniture and stuff.

The drive to Bree's house near the lakeshore should only take a couple of minutes. Over the past couple of days Derek kept waiting for her to change her mind. But between Mr. Forbes's numerous meetings and Bree's own busy tour schedule he hadn't caught sight of her alone for more than a few seconds here and there. He figured that was in his favor. He hadn't had the opportunity to piss her off again.

When he'd texted her this morning he'd half-expected her to decline his help. She hadn't, and they'd settled on a meeting time of nine o'clock. After a long run along Jake Chapman's trails before sunrise, he'd hopefully worked off any possible frustration that might come later.

He wanted to spend time with Bree, which should have struck him as strange in and of itself. He did have to make up for the way he'd acted on that house tour with her. Plus, his offer on the house had been accepted by the seller so he wanted to take her to dinner. As long as he didn't do something to fuck it all up again.

He couldn't resist driving past what would be his new

home. If anyone had told him a year ago that he'd be putting down roots in a touchy-feely place like Cypress Corners he would have called them a fool. He'd always pictured himself in a big loft condominium in Boston. The kind with floor to ceiling windows and exposed brick and beams. He'd never envisioned anything more than that bare-bones existence, though. His apartment had been leased and not really very grand. Just a place to flop over the past three years he'd been working at Chapman. Not that Bill hadn't paid him very well. He had. Not that Derek's retainer going forward wasn't sufficient either. It was. No, he just hadn't given much thought to where he'd slept.

He supposed that might be because he'd been saving everything he could in case his mother needed it. He'd wanted her completely independent from his father, but he'd overseen the drafting of her divorce and he'd made sure the bastard would continue to pay through the nose for years to come.

Last year, while in a hot debate with his mother over that impending divorce, he'd been preoccupied during his visit with Eli to Cypress. Almost upon arriving this time, though? This time he'd opened his eyes to more than the possibility of finding his mother a new place. He'd focused on finding his own, outside of Boston and outside of his father's influence.

He parked the truck in front of what would be his new house. Its pale blue clapboard siding looked a little worn out, but a fresh coat of paint on the outside would do a lot. Maybe he'd go a little darker, and have the trim painted a bright white. Do the front doors in a glossy deep red. Give it a real New England feel.

Bree was right about the huge front porch. He could imagine his mother and sister hanging out there, in wicker or Adirondack chairs. Maybe a glider or swing. The front entry was massive, and the large carriage lights on either side of the double front doors were scaled to fit the size. He'd be moving in before the month was out, if the closing date lined up with what he'd requested. Then he would have a place his mother would feel safe.

His house was a lot like Bree's, at least in style if not in size. Traditional with sturdy squared-off columns that held up the roof and led the eye to the deep eaves. Two of the three upstairs bedrooms overlooked the backyard like the first-floor guest suite but the master bedroom boasted a balcony set over the front porch. It was a little unusual, but with the temperate weather in Central Florida he imagined he'd use that balcony more often than not.

Resisting the urge to go up onto the front porch to peer into the windows like a little kid, he drove on towards Bree's house. Her street wasn't far from the Cypress Inn, which was why he'd walked over there the other evening. She'd looked so sweet sitting there, wrapped in that thick blanket. She'd been watching the sunset and he'd taken a few seconds to watch her. She'd looked…soft. More like the girl he'd held in his arms in his soon-to-be kitchen and less like the one he'd known before or since.

Giving himself a mental shake, he parked the truck, got out and walked up to her front porch. As he raised his fist to knock she opened the door.

"Good morning!" She practically hummed as she stepped out onto the porch, glancing over his shoulder behind him. "Ooh, Eli's truck. Good."

He pulled back to take her in. She wore jeans that ended midcalf and a white baseball shirt with pink sleeves. With sneakers on her feet and her hair pulled back in a ponytail, she looked more like a college coed than the successful salesperson he knew her to be.

"You look ready to hit it," he said.

She bounced a little on the balls of her feet as she fingered the strap on the bag slung over one shoulder. "I really don't know what to expect to find in there, but I'm hoping it'll be something to make this place feel more homey."

He nodded and waved her ahead of him. "Lead on. I'm your pack mule today."

She smiled at him, a big smile that nearly knocked him off his feet. "Then tonight's dinner will be on me."

He arched a brow as he opened the passenger door for her. "We're going to finally have dinner?"

"Finally?" She hopped up into the seat. "We've known each other for less than a week."

He smiled at that. "It's been some week. First you kiss me and then you avoid me."

She gasped and he went around to the driver's side.

"You kissed me!"

"All right. You slapped me."

She bit her lower lip, obviously holding back another smile as she buckled her seatbelt. "You have me there."

He buckled himself and started the engine. "Just tell me to drive, Bree."

"On to Orlando, Derek."

He nodded and pulled away from the curb. "This should be

an interesting day."

"Oh? Why?"

"I bet whatever your grandmother left you will say a lot about her." He risked a glance at her as he pulled onto the main street. "And about you."

***

Bree settled back into the soft leather seats as she mulled over Derek's statement. "Am I that big a mystery? I thought you said you knew women like me."

He visibly winced. "Yes, I did say that."

She gave a deep nod. "I believe you added that you've had women like me?"

"Look, I said I was a dick. Can we leave it at that?"

She laughed a little. "Sounds about right to me."

He shot her a challenging look, and faced front again. He was dressed casually today, like he had been that night he'd walked over to make his apology. Worn jeans, sneakers, and a soft-looking long-sleeved T in moss green. The sleeves were pushed up, and she couldn't help but gaze at his strong arms again. This was Derek Stone. Prickly, stick-up-his-butt Derek Stone.

She told herself she'd forgotten how those arms had felt

around her. Convinced herself that she'd put their kiss out of her mind. But his scent surrounded her in the closed truck cab, and all of those memories wound around her. Judging by the stupid flutter in her pulse, she hadn't forgotten a thing.

"I never would have taken Eli for a truck guy," he said after a while.

"Nobody was more surprised than Caro when her husband bought this truck," she said. "Eli jumped into life at Cypress with both feet."

Derek nodded. "Seems like he did."

"That's what you want, I think. To jump into life here."

A quick turn of his head in her direction showed her his brows were drawn together before smoothing into his usual cool expression. "Why do you say that?"

"You put in an offer on the first house you saw, Derek."

"I put in an offer on the first house you showed me, Bree. I'd already searched the database for everything that was available and settled on that one before we'd even climbed into the golf cart."

"You did?"

He shrugged one of those broad shoulders of his. "Due diligence."

That was the second time he'd mentioned those words. "Okay, Due Diligence."

"Please don't call me that," he said with a chuckle.

"All right, then. Boston."

He shook his head. "Not that either, please."

"But you are so Boston."

"What does that even mean? Eli is from there too, you know."

"Yeah, but Eli is from the city part. The Chapman part."

"And me?"

"You're from the older part, I think. The big houses near the water part."

"Okay, I'll give you that."

She nodded. They didn't speak much after that little exchange, except for her to give him directions to the storage place. It was just north of Orlando, so the drive took them nearly an hour. He parked the truck in front of the unit she indicated.

Staring at the corrugated metal door, she slowly took in a breath. Her heart was hammering now, and this time it had nothing to do with the guy sitting next to her in the truck.

"What's wrong?" Derek asked.

She turned with a jerk. "Um, nothing. I guess I'm just

wondering what my grandmother left me."

He pulled the keys out of the ignition and sat back. "Only one way to find out."

She rubbed her palms over her thighs. "Okay, Due Diligence. Let's go."

He shook his head at the nickname but his smile was unexpected. They both got out of the truck and stood in front of the door of the unit.

"This is one of the big ones," he said. "Do you need to check in at the office or anything?"

"No." She reached into her bag and withdrew the key. It dangled from a fuzzy purple tassel that was so Grandmother. "I've been hanging on to this for a while."

Her hand shook a little as she grasped the thick metal lock.

"Here, let me." Derek held the lock while she fit the key into it. "Is it stuck?"

She wiggled it a little and it scraped home. Derek held the lock tight as it popped open. Her stomach tumbled as she stepped back from the lock.

Derek gave her a curious look and reached down to grab the door handle near the ground. "Ready?"

Swallowing around the lump in her throat, she gave a

shaky nod. With a groan and a grinding of metal on metal, the door rumbled up and overhead. With a flick of the switch just inside the space, fluorescent lights illuminated the unit.

"Whoa."

Derek's one-word exclamation echoed her very thoughts. The unit was stacked to the ceiling with boxes and wrapped paintings and mirrors. As she ran her gaze over the contents she recognized a few of the pieces of furniture neatly fit against each other. Trunks filled with goodness knew what, crates and more boxes, and lamps and artwork all demanded her attention. It was a little overwhelming.

"I guess I'd better get started," she said.

"I'm your muscle today, Bree."

That made her smile a little. "Brains and brawn, huh? Are you sure?"

"Hey, I work out. I even hit the trails this morning."

"Okay, okay." She placed her hands on her hips and stared at the neatly-arranged puzzle of possessions. "Let's dig in."

Derek moved the larger pieces out of the way and she debated over which ones to take back to her house. She pointed out a few of the lamps, both very deco and done in a brass that had gone dark with age. The shades were thick glass and in shades of rose and plum.

"Those are…different," Derek said.

"Those are heirlooms, my friend. My great, great grandmother's." She saw that the bed of Eli's truck was lined with gray quilted moving blankets. "Where did you get those?"

"I thought you might need them so I went to the office while you were digging through those boxes."

He'd obviously meant the crates of dishes and crystal. Her house wasn't ornate in any way shape or form, but having a few quality pieces that reminded her of her grandmother would be very welcome.

"Thanks."

He nodded and lifted the floor lamps and one of the large mirrors she'd unearthed. "You can't possibly mean to take all of this today."

She laughed a little. "Maybe if I bought your new house it might fit, but no. I would like a few pieces to start fitting my old life into my new one, though."

He set the items carefully in the truck and straightened. "Your old life?"

Oops, she'd said too much. There would be questions. Guys always asked questions. What was it like growing up in

Heathrow with a wealthy family? What was her father like? How much is he worth? Why don't you work for your family's business? Like she would ever go into insurance. Yes, she sold Cypress Corners like nobody's business, but she wasn't selling a product that was only worth something when the buyer was gone. No. She was selling a way of life, and a way to live it to the fullest with the people they loved.

She hardly ever saw her parents, outside of over-the-top holiday parties where she was summoned to attend. She preferred to think that she'd sprung from the earth fully formed at the age of twenty-five, but she had ties to her family that no amount of time or space would loosen.

"Sorry, just thinking out loud."

He smirked at her and she could help but smile. It wasn't just the expression that looked so out of place, though. No. His hair was mussed and his chiseled cheeks were streaked with grime and dust.

"What are you staring at?" he asked.

"Do I look as funny as you do?"

He jumped down from the truck bed and looked down at himself, brushing at his rumpled and dusty clothes. "I think the word you're looking for is dirty."

She didn't think he meant to sound seductive, but her silly body sure took it that way. When his gaze traveled over the front of her equally-filthy clothes she couldn't stop herself from reacting physically. Her nipples tightened and her pulse raced.

"Derek." Her voice sounded reedy but she attributed that to the dust floating around them. "Don't."

He stepped closer. "Don't what?"

Retreating into the storage unit, she backed up until she was pressed against her grandmother's heavy mahogany hope chest. "Don't kiss me."

He came really close to her, staring down at her with dark eyes. "What makes you think I'm going to kiss you?"

She licked her lips and watched as his parted on a soft curse. "You're looking at me like you want to."

He gave a slow nod. "Ah, I want to."

"You do?" That breathiness was in her voice again.

"But I don't want another slap."

Would she slap him? No. "I didn't slap you because you kissed me."

"True."

"Maybe I won't if you kiss me again."

His brows arched and a slow smile curved his lips. "No?"

She corralled her meager strength against his appeal and placed her hand in the middle of his very strong chest. "I said maybe."

"Looks like I'll have to do my due diligence."

"How?"

"Research, Bree."

A rush of lust crashed over her. "Research."

"I'll keep you posted on my progress."

His words were so starchy and completely at odds with the soft and sensual expression on his face that she couldn't help but laugh. He joined her, the sound low and rumbly.

"Now quit stalling," he said. "We have work to do."

She pushed away from the chest and straightened, coming within a hairsbreadth of the pecs beneath her palm. "Work now." She couldn't resist giving him a pat. "Research later."

Chapter 6

Derek groaned and his whole body stiffened for a hot minute. "There's a challenge there."

She shrugged, her blue eyes sparkling. God, she was a puzzle. Holding his hands up, he stepped back from her. His chest itched where her hand had just been, and he refrained from running his own down the front of himself.

"Then let's get a move on," he added.

She turned and bent down to open the chest behind her. He looked at her ass for a while, he was a guy and she had a great ass, before heading over to the opened crates of dishes and stuff.

"So do you want to bring all of these dishes back to your house?"

"Yes, please," she said absently. "I'll go through the crates back at my house. We can stash them in my garage."

The crates were filled with that excelsior stuff that was like shredded wood or paper. She'd pulled some of it out and a few of the plates were jumbled.

"For somebody so OCD you sure left a mess in here."

"OCD?" She tilted her head, her ponytail slipping to one side. "Are you calling me anal?"

"It's just that you're usually so put together." He ran his

gaze over her smudged clothes and the excelsior tangled in her hair. "Although, right now? Not so much."

Her cheeks flushed as pink as her shirt sleeves. "I'm a working girl. Or did you not pick up on that, Due Diligence?"

He'd stuck his foot in it, apparently, but he wasn't quite sure how. He sure didn't want her pissed at him. Again.

"I know you work hard, Bree. I just meant that you always look so pressed and proper."

One pale brow arched and her full lips pursed. "Pressed and proper? You've been watching too much PBS."

He laughed at that. Actually, he realized he laughed more around her over the past few days than he'd laughed over the past year.

"I come from Bah-ston, as you said. I know proper."

She leaned against the open chest and crossed her arms. "Yes, you have that written all over you. What, exactly, is your background?"

"Nope. I'm not telling you mine until you tell me yours."

"And that is so not happening."

"You, Bree James, are a woman with a past."

That made her smile. "You can't get it out of me, counselor."

He mirrored her stance. "I'm willing to bet you'd break on the cross."

"And tell you everything? Keep dreaming."

"Another challenge?"

She ran her hands over her hair and took a breath. "You're a little infuriating, do you know that?"

"Honestly, no one has ever called me that before."

"That is surprising."

"I'll let you have that one."

"Giving me the point?"

"Is this a game?"

Her gaze ran over him and he felt it like a long, slow stroke. His jeans grew a little tight but his untucked shirt probably hid any evidence that might incriminate him.

"I don't play, Derek. Ever."

"Now that is a shame."

They worked in relative silence after that little exchange. He got her to agree to let him buy lunch, and they shared a meal of drive-through burgers and fries. After that, Derek just did whatever she instructed. Move this. Open that. Tote that barge, lift that bale. He smiled to himself as yet another nautical reference clanged through his brain. Back when he'd first learned to sail, he had the most fun going out with his uncle Jackson.

His mother's brother was a lot of laughs, and one of the reasons Derek liked him so much was that the man was nothing like his father. He came from as much privilege and money as Eddie but he wore it like a comfortable sweater instead of a straightjacket. It was only after Eddie had heard Derek praising him one too many times that he'd taken over Derek's tutelage. That was a dark day, as far as he was concerned. Derek had been about eight years old.

Eddie was no teacher. He was a taskmaster. A tyrant. He would make Derek do a task over and over until he got it right, using verbal and sometimes physical abuse to get his particular points across.

Derek brushed the dust off of his palms and glanced down at his hands. His skin still bore the scars of Eddie's lessons. He'd lost count of how many times he'd coiled and uncoiled the ropes on that day. The cold, rain-slick hemp had sliced at his small hands but Eddie hadn't cared. His tender palms had blistered, scabbed, and split again and again.

The argument his parents had later that night had been horrific. His mother had railed at Eddie for hurting Derek and his father had argued that "the little pussy" had to toughen up. As he held Abby close to him—she'd come to his room during the night—he'd silently vowed to toughen up. To get tough enough to hit Eddie back. It would take eight more years, but the first time he'd punched his father it had been the last. Until last year, that was. Last year he'd punched him and taken him to the cleaners.

"I guess that's it for now," Bree said.

She stood near the truck, her eyes on the interior of the storage unit. It was still filled to the gills.

"Are you sure?"

She shrugged and rubbed a hand over her cheek. More dirt streaked her face now. "I can always come back. It'll take me some time to go through the crates anyway."

"Just let me know and I'll fetch and carry again."

"You don't have to do that, Derek."

"I know."

She searched his face but he had no idea what she was looking for. It didn't really matter, since he was so good at keeping any hint of true expression hidden.

"Thank you." She brightened beneath the dirt and dust. "I just might take you up on that."

He helped her close up and tidy the unit a little and then made sure everything was secure in the bed of the truck. She hadn't picked out any big pieces, other than that carved chest. It wasn't long before she was locking up the place with that funny purple-tasseled key. It was nearly three o'clock. He couldn't remember the last time he'd spent a whole day with a woman who wasn't his sister or mother.

"So how about that dinner?" he asked as he turned the truck back towards Cypress.

"You're on." She held up a hand. "But only if you still want to after helping me tote this stuff into my garage."

"I wouldn't bet against that."

***

Bree walked into the Town Tavern with Derek close behind her. He'd returned Eli's truck after their heavy lifting and insisted on driving to dinner in his Lexus. She'd admitted, to herself at least, that his car was pretty sweet. Then again, she was kind of partial to automotive flash.

The girl at the hostess stand, Becky Rollins' sister Joy, smiled at her and raised her eyebrows comically when she spied Derek. He did look really good tonight, wearing his own brand of upscale casual. His khaki chinos fit just right and his white button-down shirt boasted the thinnest blue lines. He wore suede oxfords but somehow managed to look just this side of stuffy.

It was after six on a Saturday, and the place was filling up. Most of the people she worked with came here, either to grab a surprisingly-good pizza to go or a bag of burgers. They did a pretty good salmon and their salads were inspired. It sure beat the heck out of the Clubhouse, which was adjacent. It was way too upscale for her comfort and reminded her of stifling dinners with her parents.

"This is a pretty popular place," Derek said as they took up a spot to wait for their table.

"Not much choice in Cypress, I'm afraid. Not in the evening, anyway."

"I've only grabbed take-out from here. No room service at the inn."

She nodded. Ugh, small talk. This felt very date-y, given his clothes and the fact that she'd slipped into a sleeveless dress covered in watercolor flowers and a pair of sandals. She really didn't want to think about it that way, though. She was repaying him for all of his help, and God help him if he tried to pay the check. What's wrong with a girl wanting to look nice on a Saturday night, right?

Joy waved them over and they followed her to a small two-top set near the stone fireplace. The tavern was styled to resemble an English pub and it had a cozy feel the Clubhouse couldn't begin to project. Dark wood paneling, green-shaded lights, not to mention the fireplace, made the restaurant feel relaxed and intimate at the same time. The resemblance to a date intensified but she soldiered on, draping her thin pink cardigan on the back of the chair before settling down on it.

"Your server will be right with you," Joy said. "Meanwhile, can I get you two anything to drink?"

Derek raised his brows to Bree, obviously letting her order first. "A glass of pinot, please Joy."

"Sam Adams."

Joy left and Bree raised her brows at him now. "Sam Adams?"

"Hey, you can take the guy out of Bah-ston…"

She laughed, feeling herself relax a little. "I can't tell you how much I appreciate all of your help today, Derek."

"I don't know how thankful you'll be as you go through all of those boxes stacked in your garage."

"Baby steps. I'm not in any hurry to unpack everything."

"How long have you lived in your house?"

"About a year now."

"And you haven't unpacked?" His smile was crooked.
"Baby steps is right."

She waved a hand. "I unpacked. I just didn't have a lot of stuff. Just clothes and a few dishes and stuff."

"You traveled light then."

It wasn't a question but it made her stop and think for a second. She fingered the string of pearls at her neck. "I guess I did."

Joy dropped their drinks at their table and hurried back to the hostess stand.

Derek turned his pilsner glass on the table top. "I didn't bring much with me from Boston, either."

"You have a whole lot more house to fill than I do."

"It won't just be me." He looked like he was going to say more, but then he gave an almost imperceptible shake of his head. Did he have a girlfriend who would be joining him in Cypress? He didn't act like a guy with a girlfriend. Not when he was kissing her lips off.

"Maybe you can come with me to pick out some furniture," he said, dragging her mind away from that kiss.

"That's really Jessie's thing," she said. "She's the one who stages the models, primarily."

"She does a good job. The model you showed me last week felt like a home."

"That's her specialty. Although I'm surprised you noticed anything during that tour."

"Why?"

"Derek, you ran through there like your hair was on fire."

He blinked at her, then his expression cleared. "I had a lot of things on my mind. I'm sorry if I was rude."

"Another apology?" The guy was racking them up all right.

He shrugged in answer, but she suspected he was going to say he was sorry again. They each opened their menus and focused on that for a while. The server, a tall kid she thought also worked at the town market, came and took their orders. A burger for him and the pulled chicken sandwich for her.

Derek took a sip of his beer and set it back down. "Have you decided where you want to put that humongous chest?"

"It's a hope chest, I'll have you know."

"Your grandmother had a whole lot of hope."

"A joke? Derek, are you turning all charming on me?"

"Just making conversation, Bree."

"Then thank you again for carrying that inside for me."

He snorted and lifted his pilsner glass in a toast. "To no more thanks."

She caught his meaning in a flash and raised her glass in answer. "To no more apologies."

He opened his mouth, and then nodded. "You have a deal."

Talk during dinner felt a lot looser to her. When the check came, she flattened her hand over the black vinyl folder.

"No way, buddy. You might not let me thank you again but there's no way I'm letting you pay for dinner tonight."

He leaned his elbows on the table. "That's fair. As long as you let me return the favor at a future date."

"A date?" She shook her head. "Oh, I'm not sure about that."

"All right, then. At a future time to be set and approved by both parties."

She laughed. "Wow, you sound just like a lawyer."

He spread his hands. "This is surprising to you?"

Shaking her head, she tucked her card into the folder. "Not really. I was surprised when…never mind. It's none of my business."

"What isn't any of your business?"

She took a breath. "You said earlier that it wouldn't be just you in the house."

"I did." She arched a brow at him and he seemed to catch on. "Ah, I don't have a girlfriend. If that's what you were thinking."

"I was, actually."

He leaned closer, his lips curved slightly. "If I had a girlfriend I never would have kissed you like that."

"No?"

He shook his head. "And if I had a girlfriend there's no way I'd be thinking about kissing you right now."

That little confession made her body flush hot. "Derek," she whispered.

He just looked at her with those dark eyes. When the server brought the check back a minute later her hand was trembling as she signed it. She had to rein in this craziness. He might not have a girlfriend, true. But he was so not right for her.

If that were true, then why was she thinking about that kiss and the one that might come next?

Chapter 7

Derek felt a little ragged around the edges as he placed his hand on the small of Bree's back. Her pretty dress was as soft as it looked and he let his touch linger for a few seconds before pulling his hand away. She might not be aware of it but he'd shared more with her than he'd ever shared with a woman. Hell, it was more than he'd ever shared with anybody really.

The girl Bree seemed to know, Joy, smiled as they neared the hostess stand. "How was everything?"

Bree squared her shoulders and smiled. "Very good."

"Yes, thank you," Derek added.

"How long have you been working here, Joy?" Bree asked.

The brunette shook her head. "I've been exiled here in Cypress, so I'm taking whatever work I can get. I've been at the tavern for just over a month."

Bree nodded. "Text me. It sounds like we need to have a coffee date. Soon."

"Will do," Joy said. "Have a good night."

Derek held the door open for Bree and followed her out into the night. His Lexus was parked on the street, which was pretty much impossible back in Boston. The air was much chillier than it had been earlier, and he saw goosebumps rise on her skin. Reaching for the sweater draped over her arm, he held it as she slipped into it. Her hair brushed over the back of his hands and he lifted it out of the collar of her sweater before stepping back.

"Thank you" she said, looking at him over her shoulder.

He shook his head. "No more thanks. Remember?"

Her eyes sparkled up at him. "Yeah, yeah."

He held the car door open for her and she slid gracefully onto the leather seat. Her dress rode up a little and he took a long look at her legs before closing the door. Very nice. He knew her skin was soft. And her muscles were firm. He'd stroked the back of her thighs that day in his new house. He'd held her close and tasted that saucy mouth of hers.

Putting that out of his head, he got behind the wheel. "So the 'no date' rule. That's only for me?"

"What?"

"You told that Joy girl you would have a coffee date with her."

"That's different."

"Different how?"

"Joy and I have never kissed."

He managed to keep from smiling at her answer as he

started the car. "Hmm."

"You're thinking about it, aren't you?"

He pulled away from the curb and headed toward her house. "I'm a guy, Bree. Hell yes, I'm thinking about it. Now that, I won't apologize for."

She gave him a sexy smirk and he drove on. Her friend Joy might be cute but compared to Bree? Bree had his every attention and a woman hadn't been able to pull that one on him in a long time.

He stopped in front of her house and she was out of the car almost before he switched off the engine. Taking long strides, he met up with her on her front porch. She finally stopped, turning to him with her shoulders visibly rigid. The carriage lights on the porch must have been motion activated, because they snapped on and made her hair look like golden silk.

"This was nice, Derek."

"Nice." He shook his head. "I suppose it was."

Her brows drew together. "What's wrong with nice?"

"Nothing." He stepped closer. "Nice is just that. I'm hoping for more than that going forward."

"Going forward?"

He could smell her now, as he had in the car. That floral

scent he'd caught on that rainy morning just last week. "This is just starting, Bree."

"What, Derek?" She licked her lips. "What's just starting?"

"This. Us."

"Us?"

He reached out to stroke a finger over her delicate collar bone. Goosebumps rose again, but he knew they had nothing to do with the chill. "I want to see you."

"I'm not dating right now."

He noticed that she didn't back away from his touch.

"Fine," he said. "Call it what you want."

"Oh no, you don't. You might be a lawyer but trust me. This isn't an argument you can win."

He growled softly and watched as her pupils dilated. "I like being around you, Bree. Tell me you don't feel the same thing?"

"That's just chemistry."

"That's fair game, then. Let's go inside and talk about it."

She placed her hand on his chest like she had before. He wondered if she realized she was slowly stroking him even as she was pushing him away.

"Derek, I'm just starting my life."

"One crate at a time."

She shrugged. "Maybe."

"Hey, I just got to Cypress. I'm not ready for any entanglements either."

"Are you suggesting we just scratch the itch?"

He shook his head. "No. If I wanted that I'd just go hook up with somebody."

"You don't want to hook up?"

He slid her a slow grin. "I'm not saying that."

"I like my job. I'm good at it."

"Don't tell me that Cypress has an anti-fraternization policy, Bree. I'm in-house counsel, remember?"

That earned him a small smile. "Okay, you've got me there."

He stepped closer. The porch was covered, and her house was situated on the corner. There were no neighbors adjacent to where they stood, and he took advantage of the privacy.

"Invite me in for coffee, Bree."

"Just coffee?"

"Lady's choice. At least I can give you some ideas on where to put that hope chest."

She turned and unlocked the front door. "Boy, I'd sure hate to come up against you in court."

"I practice purely corporate law, I'm afraid. But don't worry. I can argue a contract until the sun comes up, baby."

She pushed the door open. "Color me surprised."

As he stepped in behind her she flicked on the can lights in the big kitchen's ceiling. Her house was a lot like his soon-to-be home on the inside, too. There was a huge lack of furniture not to mention photos and artwork. A stack of take-out menus on the back counter of the kitchen told him she didn't cook much and, while the new couch looked comfortable, there really wasn't much about the place that made it feel like a home.

"You've lived here a year?" he asked.

"I know." She sighed and placed her hands on her hips. "I've been living in limbo."

"Yes, but the weather's nice."

Her eyes widened. "You're making another joke? You are a puzzle, Derek Stone."

He knew he was. It was part of his personality, honed through years of self-preservation. He revealed only as much as he wanted to. He never let his father see that he was hurt. He never let his mother know how upset he was. He always presented an image of the cool and collected corporate attorney. That didn't stop him from wanting to get hot and sweaty with

Bree James, though.

"You really want a cup of coffee?" she asked him.

He let his mask slip just enough to show her what he really wanted. Her. "No."

***

Bree's throat tightened. Desire was clear on Derek's face. His eyes somehow grew darker. His jaw tightened and his nostrils flared.

"I think you can guess what it is I want, Bree."

Yeah, she could. She was a grown woman. She could admit to herself that his sharply focused attention made her crave all sorts of things she'd only imagined before. This wasn't just an itch to be scratched. Nope. This was full-on lust, something she'd never felt before.

"We can't do this, Derek. It's a bad idea."

"There's nothing keeping us apart."

She swallowed and gave a weak nod. "At the moment, no."

"Then let's just be in the moment. God knows I never do that." He grasped her arms and his touch was just right. Intense yet not confining. "Ever."

She reached up to touch those thick dark waves of his, finding them cool beneath her fingers. "Ever?"

He grabbed her hand and pulled it to his mouth, placing an open-mouthed kiss on her palm. "Be in the moment, Bree."

Heat rushed up her arm from his kiss, sending sparks over her chest and throat. This was a guy who never did anything by half measure. She'd heard about his legal reputation. His career as a driven, focused corporate lawyer. What would it be like to have all of that energy centered on her?

Turning her hand, she ran her thumb over his lower lip. His mouth felt strong. Smooth and hot. She came up on her toes and brought her mouth close to his, breathing him into herself.

"Kiss me, Derek."

He groaned and covered her mouth with his. This kiss was as hot as their first, but so much more urgent. It was a kiss with intent and for the first time in her memory she let go of any worries or expectations and leaned into him.

His tongue stroked hers just right and she grabbed onto his shoulders. He turned and pressed her against the low back counter of her pretty kitchen and deftly lifted the skirt of her dress. His teeth grazed her neck as he murmured words she couldn't make out. Moving his big body against her, he lifted her onto the counter and pressed between her legs.

"Oh!" She leaned her head back as he kissed her throat.

"Derek."

Her sweater was gone, she wasn't sure how. With the thin straps of her dress pushed down off of her shoulders, he placed his mouth on one of her breasts. Her nipple tightened as her lacy bra grew wet. Her heart raced as she closed her eyes, loving what he was doing to her.

"Let go, Bree." His hand was between her spread thighs now, stroking and rubbing as he ratcheted up the tension coiling inside of her. "Come, baby." His voice was low and rough. "Come for me."

He drew hard on her nipple as one finger moved past the crotch of her panties to slip inside of her. She clenched around him as her climax struck. She could hear herself crying her release, her body jerking as he kept up the pressure for several more blissful moments.

Her breath hitched and his was labored.

He dropped a sweet kiss on her breast and brought his brow to hers. "Are you okay?"

Drawing in a deep breath, she nodded. "More than okay."

His laugh was a surprise. Opening her eyes, she saw his eyes twinkling even as his features were held tight. "Good."

He removed his hand and pressed close against her damp

center. "You feel more than okay, too."

"You feel like you might need a little something."

"I'm a big boy, Bree." He stepped back, hissing out a breath as he adjusted his khakis. "I'll have a lot to think about later."

An image popped into her head, of him thinking about her as he stroked himself to release. Maybe in the luxurious bathroom she knew the rooms at the inn possessed. Another flash of heat danced over her.

Pushing at her skirt, she brought her still-trembling legs together and fixed the straps of her dress. Derek helped her down from the counter and crossed his arms.

"So tell me. What's to stop us from seeing where this goes?"

"Where this goes?" She brushed her hair back from her face and shook her head. "It can't go anywhere."

He didn't seem to take her seriously. His eyes were warm now and his sexy smirk was back. "Why not?"

"I'm not going to fall for the first hot guy to ring my bells."

He gave her a cocky grin. "I rang your bells, did I?"

"You know you did."

"True."

His gaze ran over her and she stifled another shiver. "But we're not starting this."

"Evidence would show otherwise."

"You're not a trial attorney."

"No, I'm not. But that doesn't mean I don't know how to win an argument."

She had no answer to that. "Good night, Derek."

He surprised her with a sweet kiss before straightening again. She watched him walk to the front door before he turned back to her. "I can keep a secret, Bree. I've had a lifetime of practice."

With that confounding statement he left, shutting the door tight behind him.

"Whoa." She grabbed a glass out of the closest cabinet and pressed it against the fridge to fill it with water. Downing it in gulps, she let the chill cool her from the inside.

What was she going to do? She didn't want to start anything but he was right. He'd rung her bells, bells long silent or just weakly tinkling in the past. Loud, clanging bells that drove her crazy in the best way? That was what Derek had done tonight.

Closing her eyes, she recalled how good being in the

moment had felt. With him. He'd said he could keep secrets. Did she want to find out if that was true? Yes. She did.

"I'm so screwed," she whispered.

Chapter 8

Derek nodded as he looked over the signed paperwork. Jessie Brady had brought him the latest contract for his final review on this Wednesday morning, and stood fidgeting in front of his desk. He was given an office in the Sales Center next to Ben Chapman's on his first day, but he wasn't yet accustomed to people just walking in on him. Apparently Cypress had an open-door policy.

"This looks good," he said.

She nodded. "Good. This family is very eager to move into the green neighborhood."

"Into one of your husband's houses, you mean?"

She blinked at him. Noah Brady was the builder there, working with Ben Chapman's designs. "Of course."

"I'm joking, Jessie."

Her mouth gaped open. "I didn't know you joked."

That rankled, not that it should. He projected this chilly exterior, didn't he?

"I've been known to." He gave her a small smile. "Once in a great while."

Jessie stared at him a second longer and then laughed. "You're not the stick in the mud everybody says you are." She winced. "Not that we're talking about you."

"Jessie, relax. I know I'm the new kid at school. I'm not worried about fitting in."

"No? Because you won't have a problem with it or because you don't want to?"

He wasn't certain on that count, so he shrugged a shoulder. "You can go forward with these contracts. Let me know if you need anything else."

"I will." She grabbed up the papers. "Thanks again, Derek."

He watched as she hurried out the door, leaving it open. Resisting the urge to get up and close himself inside, he clicked through programs on his laptop until he found today's schedule. Amazingly, Mr. Forbes didn't have a meeting set for today.

Over the past week and a half that he'd been here he'd had to sit through sales meetings nearly every day. In two meetings so far this week he'd had to sit across the table from Bree and not think about how he'd driven her crazy after their date. After leaving her on Saturday night he'd let his mind play back what it had been like to touch her. To taste her. He'd come so hard he'd had to hold himself up against the marble walls of his shower at the inn.

He suspected Bree was hiding something, but who was he to push for disclosure? He was hiding any number of things himself, wasn't he? His cell phone vibrated on the desk top and he glanced over at it. It was his sister, whom he hadn't heard from since coming down here despite repeated texts and voicemails. His belly tightened and any thoughts of Bree and finding out what she was hiding flew out of his head. Grabbing the phone, he swiped and answered the call.

"Abby, what's up?"

She whistled in his ear. "Calm down, bro. You sound a little intense."

She didn't, which put him on his guard. "Sorry, but I messaged you days ago. So I'll ask again. What's up?"

"Okay, I've been putting off calling you about this."

"Is mom all right?"

"Yes! She's fine, and looking forward to coming down there in a few weeks."

"Did Eddie find out about our plans?"

Abby's silence answered his question. "I didn't tell him, Derek. I swear."

He knew in an instant what she meant. "Fuck."

"Exactly."

"Mom has been talking to Eddie." It wasn't a question. "Fuck."

"So you said. What are we going to do about it?"

"I'll just have to move her down here sooner," he said.

"Yeah, about that."

Derek closed his eyes, rubbing at a spot in the center of his forehead. "What, or do I even want to know?"

"I'm sure you don't want to know, but I wanted to ask you a favor."

His eyes popped open. "A favor? For you?"

She sighed, long and loud. "I want to come down with her."

"I thought you were sticking with the vet clinic?"

"I was."

"Wasn't the vet going to give you a chance to come on full-time?"

"He was."

His mind worked. "He's not now, is he?"

"No. The guy's girlfriend just finished veterinarian school in Grenada and wants the job."

"Grenada? You went to MIT, for God's sake."

"For my undergrad, big brother. Their veterinary program

was out of reach for this girl."

"You're ridiculously smart, Abby."

"And you're a good brother. Seriously, competition is too steep."

"You sound like you're giving up."

"For now, yeah."

Derek took a second to form his next words. "I'll keep my opinion on your career decisions to myself."

"That would be a first." Humor laced her voice. "I'll come down with Mom and see this Cypress place for myself."

"You're coming down with her?"

"Is that a problem?"

"No. I'll let you know when I close on the house."

"Wait, what? You found a place for Mom already?"

"No. The Active Adult community is just getting underway. I bought a house."

"You. Bought a house."

"Yes."

"You?"

"All right."

"Sorry bro, but I've never known you to have anything more than a place to flop. Not that your apartments aren't always very fancy and in the best parts of the city."

"Again, I'll let you know when you two can come down. Promise me you won't talk to Eddie about the house."

"I don't talk to that son-of-a-bitch, Derek."

"Good. It's better that way."

"Mom, on the other hand, met him for coffee yesterday."

His heart thudded. "Seriously?"

"Just coffee. She texted me when she was going and I kept an eye on the coffee shop. He left without her but he looked really pissed."

Derek thought for a second before making a decision. It hinged on a few conditions, which he had to straighten out right away.

"How long do you have at the vet clinic?"

"How did you know I gave my notice?"

"Because it's what I would do and you're smarter than I am."

"A compliment, too? I think I like Cypress Derek."

"Cypress Derek? You make me sound like an action figure."

She laughed, the full sound he knew and loved. "Two weeks, then."

111

"Okay, good. Keep an eye on Mom for me and let me know if she has any more contact with Eddie. Otherwise I'll see you both down here after I close on the house."

"Will do. And Derek?"

"What?"

"Thank you."

His throat tight, he just nodded even though she couldn't see it. Abby ended the call and Derek set his phone back down on the desk. What the fuck was his mother thinking, meeting with Eddie? And what did that bastard hope to accomplish? Damn it, he should have insisted his mother file that restraining order he'd drafted. Did Eddie think that Derek was too far away to convince his mother to see it through? He had better think again.

"That's not a happy face," Bree said from the doorway.

***

Derek looked up at her, his brows drawn together. "It's nothing."

It sure didn't look like nothing. "If you say so."

Derek scowled in her direction. "Did you need something?"

She stared at him, choosing to ignore the dismissal in his

tone. Something was clearly bothering him, but they didn't have any kind of relationship let alone one that would lend itself to disclosure.

"I was just going to tell you that the closing date is set."

He gave a curt nod. "When?"

"On the twenty-eighth."

"So, next week."

She nodded. "Are you sure nothing's wrong?"

He seemed to soften a little as he brushed his hair back from his brow. "Just busy, Bree."

Biting her lip, she took a chance and shut his office door. "Is it something else?"

He folded his hands on the desk and leaned forward. "*Now* my door is closed."

"What?"

He laughed without any apparent humor. "Nothing. I was on a phone call earlier."

"And you're door was open."

"Yes."

"And…that bothers you?"

"It's just a lot to get used to." He pinned her with those gorgeous eyes of his. "You know. People just popping in."

She couldn't resist teasing him a little. "Not a big fan of the pop-in?"

A flash of a smile crossed his face. "Not particularly."

"I wasn't eavesdropping, you know."

"I know."

"Do you?"

"Bree, you've avoided me since Saturday night. I don't think you would sneak around listening to my conversations."

"That's something, then."

"Was there something you wanted other than giving me the closing date?"

"No."

"Really?" He stood, slowly coming around his desk. "Because you could have texted me the information."

She stood her ground but was quickly regretting closing that door. "I could have."

Heat flared in his eyes for a second. "Then why didn't you?"

She tried to remain indifferent but even *her* masking skills were nothing compared to this guy's. "I wanted to see you."

That earned her a wide smile that changed his entire expression. "I won't gloat."

She laughed lightly. "That's refreshing."

He splayed a hand over his chest before stroking it down his burgundy tie. His shirt was several shades lighter, almost tan in color, and the sleeves were rolled up to expose those forearms she so enjoyed seeing.

"Are you saying I gloated Saturday night?"

Ooh, Saturday night. If he'd wanted her to blush, mission accomplished. "You were a gentleman," she admitted.

"A gentleman who made you come, Bree," he said, his voice low. "Hard, if I recall correctly."

She tucked some hair behind one ear. "Okay, fine."

"You saw me at meetings yesterday. And Monday, for that matter."

"I'll admit I wanted to talk to you." She ran her hands briskly over her linen skirt. "I felt like there was a lot left unsaid on Saturday night."

He crossed his arms, his biceps stretching his sleeves very nicely. "Such as?"

"Secrets, Derek. Just what did you mean?"

"You have your life, Bree. Your new life, I believe you called it."

"I do."

"And I'm making my own new life here in Cypress." He smiled crookedly. "Cypress Derek."

"Cypress Derek?"

"Never mind. So, separate lives."

He was close to her now, and she couldn't for the life of her remember why she was keeping him at arms-length. "Yes."

He took her hands in his. "We can keep this separate from our work lives, Bree."

"Keep what?"

He brought his face close to hers. "This…whatever this is."

"You're offering me, what? A secret affair?"

"Not an affair, since there's nobody to hurt in this agreement. Unless you're seeing someone?"

"I'm not."

"I stand firm."

"Always the lawyer."

"Yes."

"And let me guess. You've done your due diligence?

"No real mystery there, baby. I know what drives you crazy and that gives me all kinds of advantages in this arrangement."

"What if someone finds out?"

He touched her cheek, brushing the backs of his knuckles gently over her skin. "It's no big deal to me. I'll give you complete power if that happens, Bree."

She was tempted. "Complete power?"

"Your call going forward. I promise."

"No promises, please. You have a reputation, Derek. It preceded you. You're known as a relentless negotiator."

"I am. But I'm also smart enough to know when an argument isn't worth having."

"Hmm?"

"You're going to make up your own mind. I'm confident that you'll choose the chance to see where we can go. Completely on your terms."

She reached up and touched his cheek. The afternoon's scruff tickled her fingertips. "Okay. I'm in."

He sucked in a breath and then took her hand again. "Thank God."

His mask slipped a little again.

"Were you worried, counselor?"

He answered her by kissing her. Slow and deep and very arousing. His tongue in her mouth, his hands on her butt, she gave in for several toe-curling minutes.

117

Pulling back, he ran his hands over her hair. "Mmm, you're surprisingly soft under that prickly proper exterior."

She felt out of her element, which ticked her off a little but after that kiss? She'd give him this one.

"I'm home around six thirty tonight."

He leaned away from her, his upper body at least, and gave a nod. "I'll see you at six forty-five."

At his retreat, she opened the door and watched him return to stand behind his desk.

"Then we're all set for the twenty-eighth."

She hadn't been eavesdropping on Derek's phone call but she wouldn't put it past Oliver or Jessie. Stating the actual business she had with Derek couldn't hurt.

He licked his lips, his eyes flashing. "Yes, thank you."

Stepping out into the corridor, she made her way back to her desk in the large space the sales staff shared. What was she doing, starting an affair with a guy like Derek? He was cold. Stern. Yet she'd seen warmth there. Humor, even. And there was the little matter of the best kisses she'd ever received.

"I have the power," she murmured.

"What's that?" Oliver asked from his desk. His eyes were bright. "Power?"

She just grinned. "Nothing, Ollie."

She'd told Derek from the beginning that she wasn't a secret-keeper. This secret, though?

This one she'd keep for as long as she wanted.

Chapter 9

Derek walked out of his office, tamping down his excitement about the coming evening. He didn't know exactly what to expect when he showed up at Bree's house but he knew it would be amazing. That kiss against his closed door had fueled his imagination. She was good with those lips of hers.

He crossed into the town center. It looked a lot like New England in spring time, and he couldn't help but notice the flowers popping up just about everywhere. He had no idea what some of these flowers and plants were. He wasn't a city kid like Eli, but the only flowers he ever really saw were the arrangements his mother put in their grand entry or the roses in her garden behind the house.

He thought again about moving her—and his sister, apparently—into his new house. There was plenty of room in the back for her to put a garden. The entry wasn't quite as grand as in Eddie Stone's house but it was impressive as well as welcoming. Besides, she wouldn't live with him for long. Abby was another story but he'd deal with that later. Right now, he wanted to think about Bree and what might happen tonight.

He made his way over the brick sidewalk toward the market, seeing people walking around or just enjoying the late afternoon warmth. The storefronts were attached along this side of the street. First came the ice cream shop. Little kids and high schoolers were enjoying frozen treats on the wrought iron benches in front today. Next was the coffee shop. He waved to Lettie, who wore a smile as she lifted her glass of iced tea. He didn't want to engage the woman this afternoon. From what he'd heard, she could see right through a guy. There was no way he would let her see what he was thinking about Bree. The bright green awnings of Sweet Escape were next, but the bakery was closed at this hour.

He reached the market and saw that it was open for about another hour. He smiled to the tall skinny kid working the counter as he passed on his way towards the upturned crates serving as a wine display. His mother had impressed upon him the importance of never going to a person's house empty-handed. His patrician upbringing and New England propriety were both hard to deny. He had to show up at Bree's with something.

Grabbing a bottle each of pinot and merlot, he stepped up to the counter.

"Will this be all?" the kid asked.

Derek nodded. Maybe he should have picked up something

for dinner, but he was new to this secret dating thing they had going on. A guy buying a couple bottles of wine wouldn't raise brows but if he picked up take-out for two? The cat would probably be out of the bag. Eli and Jessie had both told him about the Cypress fishbowl. He sure as hell didn't want to be stuck in that glass, thanks.

A middle-aged guy looking like a broader version of the kid at the counter nodded to Derek as he left the market. The small town friendliness was everywhere and he didn't know if he would ever get used to it. It had felt weird when he'd been down here last year, but now this was his new normal.

"Thanks," he said to the guy as he left.

Oliver walked toward him, waving as he ducked into the sporting goods store up the block. He thought he'd heard that Oliver's boyfriend ran the store, but he wasn't sure. He peered into the wide windows as he passed, seeing a nice collection of running clothes and other equipment. Between the market and the other businesses in the square, a person really didn't have to ever leave Cypress Corners.

"That's a little unnerving," he said as he crossed the street back to his car.

"Good night, Derek," Rick Chapman called from where he

stood at his SUV.

"Good night."

"No plans tonight?" Rick asked.

Derek kept his expression even. "Nope."

"See you in the morning." Rick grinned. "Mr. Forbes called a meeting for nine-thirty."

"When did that happen?"

"Just about five minutes ago. It'll show up in your schedule soon, I'll bet."

"Okay, thanks."

Another complication. He and Bree would share…something tonight and then he'd have to sit across from her at the table in the conference room tomorrow morning.

The drive to Bree's house was short. After debating whether he should park out front, he decided that if anybody noticed his car they could just mind their own business.

"Yeah, right," he grumbled.

He took off his tie and tossed it on the passenger seat. Grabbing the bottles of wine, he walked up to her porch. There were a few things on the porch he hadn't noticed the last time he'd been here. Pillows set on the bench. A wide welcome mat. A fluffy wreath hanging on the yellow front door. Maybe he could ask for her help in making his new place more appealing.

That sunny yellow door opened and Bree stood there, her eyes narrowed but a smile curving her lips. She'd changed into jeans and a soft-looking long sleeve shirt in a blue nearly the color of her eyes. "Six forty-five on the dot."

He nodded. "As promised."

"Promised?" She stepped back to let him inside. "I don't remember asking for any promises, Derek."

"You're sharp." He smiled. "Right. No promises."

"Why does this sound the start of a negotiation?"

He set the bottles of wine on the tall counter and shrugged. "Let's review. No thank yous. No I'm sorries. Now no promises. This is on you, baby."

She laughed, a light sound he'd never heard from her before. It was sweet and musical and sexy as hell.

"I ordered a pizza," she said.

"Good, I'm starving." He gestured toward the cabinet drawers behind the tall counter. "Wine opener?"

She came around and handed it to him. "Why don't you chill the white?"

He opened the red. "Sure. What kind of pizza did you get?"

"Meat."

He arched a brow. "As in pepperoni? Sausage? Ham?"

"Yes on all three counts. The tavern makes an amazing pizza and I've been craving one all week."

"I was going to grab takeout for us but thought that might arouse too much suspicion. Cypress fishbowl and all."

"Yes, that darn fishbowl. So far I've managed to stay out of the net. Or something like that."

"Net's correct, but that would mean you're still in the bowl."

"Aren't we all?"

He laughed now and filled the glasses she handed him. "I never thought I'd miss the city life, but there is a level of anonymity that's lacking in Cypress."

"Too true."

She took a glass from him and swirled it a little before taking a sip. It was an unconscious motion, and certainly went with her proper country-club upbringing. He drank a bit of his, idly noting that the wine was pretty good considering he'd gotten it at the town market.

"So." He set his glass down on the counter closest to her and leaned in. "How is this going to work?"

She stared up at him, licking her plump lower lip. He wanted to bite that lip. To kiss her hard and do everything he'd fantasized about since meeting her last week. When she shook her head at him he nearly growled in frustration. Then she grinned.

"No more negotiations, counselor." She reached up to wrap her arms around his neck. "Let's just say that nothing is off the table."

He drew her closer, letting his hands slide down to cup her ass. She made a soft little moan and his heart started to pound. Then the doorbell rang and she slipped out of his arms.

"Dinner first," she said.

"First?" He brushed his hair back from his face. "I like the sound of that."

***

Bree's hands were a little unsteady as she took the pizza box from the kid on the front porch. "I tipped when I ordered."

"Thank you." The kid bobbed his head and loped back toward his golf cart.

She brought the box to the kitchen to find Derek had set the tall counter. He'd located the plates, but it wasn't like he'd snooped in her medicine cabinet or anything. It did feel a little too domestic and familiar, but since he'd given her an orgasm in this very kitchen she figured she'd let it slide. He'd gotten into her drawers, after all. She shouldn't be ticked off if he went into her cabinets.

"I've had their pizza," Derek said. "It's pretty good."

"Room service, so to speak, is one of the amenities I personally appreciate in Cypress Corners."

"Room service?"

She nodded and chose a piece of pizza for herself. "You can order just about anything from the tavern and have it delivered to your door."

"I didn't know that. Do you do that a lot?"

"Enough. For a single girl who really doesn't like to eat out alone, it's a great option to cooking."

"So you can't cook."

"I can cook. I just choose not to."

"I can't cook." He took a bite of his pizza and made a sound of satisfaction. "Meat. Good."

She laughed and ate some of her own dinner. "You can't cook at all?"

"I can make the guy things. Like broil a steak or pile lunchmeat on bread to make a sandwich."

"That last thing isn't cooking."

He shrugged, chewing on the crust as he grabbed another slice. "It's close enough. I hardly ever ate at home in Boston."

Her ears pricked. This was the first time he'd volunteered information about his life before Cypress. "No?"

"When I was a kid, yes. My mother baked but we had a cook who did everything else."

"Sounds like my parents' house."

He nodded. Their eyes caught for a second and she thought he was going to say something but then he just drank more of his wine. His expression had gone shuttered again. As they continued to eat, she took in his appearance. She'd changed after work but he clearly hadn't. His tie was gone and a couple more shirt buttons were undone but otherwise he was still starchy.

"I've started to dig through the crates," she offered.

"Find anything good?"

"It's all good. Very fine crystal and china and a whole host of things I'm probably not ever going to use."

"How about the hope chest? Did you decide where to put it?"

She glanced around the living area and shrugged. "I thought next to the fireplace might work."

He wiped his hands on a napkin and stood. "Let me go grab it now."

"Derek, you don't have to do that."

He folded his arms. "If you remember I hauled that sucker into your garage. I can pop it on the dolly and bring it in here."

She nibbled her lip. He'd already started to fold back the cuffs of his dress shirt and she was once more reminded of how strong he was. He wasn't any soft squishy kind of guy who subsisted under artificial light. There was an outdoorsy vibe she caught from him now and then, which seemed very out of place with what she knew about his background. What little she knew, that was.

She led him to the back of the house where the door to the garage was located. It was set at the back of the house, like most of the homes in Cypress. This gave the neighborhood streets a more welcoming feeling, letting the front porches take center stage instead of wide paver-stone driveways.

Derek had the hope chest on the dolly thing and wheeled it over to the fireplace. There was a window set to one side of it and she indicated that spot. He set it down with care and straightened.

"Is that okay?"

"That's great." She ran a hand over the smooth inlaid wood on the chest's top. "Thank you."

She was still standing there when he returned from putting the dolly back in the garage. In the harsh light of the storage unit she hadn't noticed how fine the piece was. It was covered in its inlaid design, geometric shapes both large and tiny combined to make a gorgeous art deco flower.

"I didn't realize it was so pretty."

He shrugged in answer. "It was full of her hopes, right?"

She smiled and turned. There was a wistfulness on his face, something she'd never seen there. "Does it remind you of something?"

"No. We had a lot of antiques in the house growing up. Maybe I saw something like it once. The design is pretty and it's obviously very valuable."

"You think so?"

"It's handcrafted, so yes. How old would you say this is?"

"I'm not sure. She married my grandfather back in the early sixties. If she had it for her engagement that makes it over fifty years old. It feels older, though."

"It's the style, I think. Probably dates it to around the twenties."

"She did love deco stuff. I put up one of the lamps we found."

He looked at the torchiere she'd placed over in one corner, the one with the purple shade. "Looks good there. So are you going to help me decorate my place?"

She scoffed. "Please. I haven't even done mine yet."

"Yes, but you're clearly procrastinating."

"Am I? Then what are you doing? Jumping the gun?"

He laughed. "I haven't bought anything yet. I'm just thinking that with my mother and sister coming down I'll need to do their rooms at least."

"Your mother and sister are going to live with you?"

He looked surprised that he'd shared that bit of information. "Uh, just for a little while."

She guessed he didn't want to disclose anything else about his private life. She sure wasn't sharing much with him, either. After another stroke of her hand over the chest's top, she stood. "Let's finish dinner."

In a flash she set aside any talk about family or heirlooms. He seemed to catch on quickly and her pulse spiked.

"Dinner first." He nodded, his eyes dark. "Right."

She walked back to the kitchen, feeling his gaze on her

now. Yes, dinner first. And then she would get to know Derek Stone a little bit better. He was letting down his guard, after all. Maybe she should return the favor. He'd given her the power, hadn't he?

Tonight she was going to use it.

Chapter 10

Derek pulled Bree close, running his hands all over her body. They were tangled on her couch, wearing very little. He'd noticed the black lace bra on Saturday night. Tonight's was in a pink color nearly the same shade as her nipples. She'd torn off his shirt and now he only wore his boxer briefs. He hadn't made out on a couch in years, but this felt just right.

She arched as he kissed her again, her hands in his hair as she drove her tongue into his mouth. She was smooth and sweet all over, and when he touched her damp lace panties he felt her heat.

"Derek," she breathed as she pulled away from his kiss. "Oh, that feels good."

He lowered his face to her cleavage, licking his way to her nipple. Her floral scent was stronger here, and he breathed her in. Her bra had a plastic hook in the front, so he released it with a flick of his fingers. She filled his hands, plump and tight, and he couldn't wait to get her skin-to-skin.

Bracing himself on his hands, he rubbed his chest against her breasts. She made a sound of pleasure and he shifted so that his groin was cradled by her thighs. There was very little between them right now, but he wasn't going to push her for more. Not yet, anyway.

"Baby, you feel so good." He kissed her again before sucking on her nipples. "Taste so good."

She arched again and he moved down to lick her through her panties.

"Oh!" She wriggled against him, obviously as hot for him as he was for her.

He moved the lace aside with one thumb and placed his mouth on her. She was slick and sweet, and he ran his tongue over her pussy with one long stroke. She trembled and he glanced up to see her close her eyes. Proper, patrician Bree was gone and this girl beneath him craved everything he wanted to give her.

"Come for me, baby." He licked and suckled her clit and she began to sob. "Let go."

She cried out, rising against him as she shivered in her release. It was like their first night, but better. Deeper. Damn, he wanted to be inside of her but they weren't there yet. Not that he had any idea of when that would be.

He pulled away from her and watched as her eyes fluttered open. He couldn't help but smile at how rosy and rocked she looked.

"Wow." She grinned up at him. "That was… Wow."

"So you said." He took her hand and tugged her to a seated position. His dick was as hard as that inlaid wood on her grandmother's hope chest, but he wouldn't pressure her. "You're okay?"

She stretched her arms up over her head and he got another great look at her tits. "Better than okay."

He nodded, trying to keep raw need from showing on his face.

"What about you?" she asked when he didn't say anything.

"I'll live."

She shook her head. "Nope. I'm not leaving you like that again."

"That?" He chuckled. "What do you mean?"

"You're hard, Derek. Ooh, you're hard and you need something."

"Damn right I do, but I gave you the power, remember?"

"Yeah, you did. Seems to me that was a rookie mistake, counselor."

She cupped him and he groaned. "You're killing me, Bree. Tell me I won't have to jerk off again tonight?"

Her hand stilled. "You really did that?"

135

He eyed her. "I did. And I was thinking about you the whole time."

She bit her lower lip and folded her legs underneath her ass. "What did you think about?"

"What you felt like that night. What you tasted like."

"Tasted?"

"I used my imagination, but tonight I realized I was way off. You're fucking delicious."

She sucked in a breath, her eyes wide. "Oh, my."

He shrugged and she cupped him through his briefs. "Bree, please."

She grinned and pushed his briefs down. "That's just what I was thinking."

He'd expected a hand job at the very least but when she put her mouth on him he nearly exploded. With every lick, every suckle, she drove him crazy. Putting his hands in her silky hair, he held her head reverently as her mouth and tongue did very naughty things to his dick.

When he couldn't hold back any longer he came. His orgasm was sharp and shook him hard. He was breathing fast as he let his head fall back. Bree curled up against his side, stroking his face as she kissed his neck. "You taste good too."

He wanted to laugh but all that came out was a damn whimper. "You killed me."

"It's fun to have the power."

He lifted his head and looked at her. Her face was rosy pink and her eyes were shining. "Feeling pretty good about yourself, aren't you?"

She nodded vigorously. "Yes I am. And I'm looking forward to the next time."

"The next time?"

"As long as we keep this between us."

It was there again. Her fear about losing the life she was starting to build here. He had his own set of baggage too, didn't he? He'd play by her rules.

"You've got it."

She kissed him again, but before he could get things going she pressed a hand against his chest. "You should go."

"I've said it before." He tucked himself back into his briefs and stood. "Lady's choice."

The look of relief on her face made something shift in his chest. They had so much in common. This was from what little he knew about her, and already he could see that. If they played by her rules, he'd never know much more. Wouldn't any guy jump at this chance, though? He sure would have if any of his hookups had made the offer. No strings. Non-dating. Whatever they called it, it would be incredible before it ended.

He set that depressing thought from his mind and dressed. She pulled on her shirt and jeans, but he couldn't help but notice that she wasn't wearing the bra. He stared at her nipples poking at the cotton before dragging his gaze back to her face.

"Thanks for dinner, Bree. I'll get the next one."

"Okay."

She walked him to the door and he couldn't help kissing her good night. Her hair was mussed and her cheeks still rosy. She looked soft and sexy and he didn't want to leave. That was a first for him, so he placed his hand on the doorknob.

"Good night," he said.

"Good night."

She shut the door and he walked to his car. Something had changed between them tonight. Talking about his mother and sister moving down? That had shocked him. She'd seemed curious but he couldn't tell her more. Then he'd have to tell her about Eddie and the many times Derek had failed to keep his mother safe.

That was something he wasn't going to share with

anybody, not even the girl who drove him out of his mind with just a kiss.

***

Bree sat in the model home two days later, humming to herself as she thumbed through the emails on her tablet. Jessie's husband Noah was working in the office at the back of the house, but she didn't mind giving him that space. She was on domestic detail, as she often thought of the "living with the house" assignment.

A married couple she guessed were in their thirties were murmuring back and forth as they toured the house on their own. They visited the kitchen again and she simply smiled at them. She had given them the welcoming spiel and then let them have at it. In her experience, they were much more likely to picture themselves in a home if there wasn't a salesperson dragging them around.

This was most likely her last showing of the day. Of the week, really. It was Friday, after all.

She'd managed to keep herself from smiling like an idiot when she'd run into Derek in the breakroom yesterday, but she suspected it was only a matter of time before she said or did something to bring attention to their little non-affair. Wednesday night had been amazing. She'd never felt like that before. Free and sexy. He'd driven her crazy and she'd returned the favor.

That had been a first for her. Taking enjoyment in it, at least. In college guys seemed to expect that and it had been a way to placate them just to get them the hell out of her room. Pleasing Derek, though? It made her feel powerful. Naughty, too. Free, somehow.

The couple came into the kitchen again. By the raised eyebrows and expectant vibe, she knew they were sold.

"I just love it!" the wife said.

"Do you have the list of what's an upgrade in this model?" the man asked, obviously trying to rein in his wife's enthusiasm.

He didn't have to worry. They didn't push for sales in Cypress. Nope. They simply brought the horse to water, so to speak. The drinking? That was all on them. Luckily, Cypress had a way of making them thirsty.

"You have choices of finishes, naturally," Bree said. "But nothing you've seen here is an upgrade. Aside from the pool out back, of course."

The wife nodded vigorously. "Well, I just love it." She laughed a little. "I keep saying that."

"Yeah, you do," the husband grumbled with a small smile.

Bree handed them the folder she'd put together for them, including items tailored to their particular wants. School info, for example. They had kids, after all.

"This model is set to be built on the lots I've indicated on the neighborhood map," she said. "If you have specific questions regarding the building materials I can put you touch with the builder, Noah Brady."

The wife's smile widened. "We met him! He's so nice."

Bree nodded. Noah was getting used to interacting with homeowners, and she suspected that was Jessie's influence on him.

"You have my email. Please email me if you have any questions." She arched one brow. "You do know that the Sales Center and models are closed on the weekends."

"We do," the husband said. "I like that. It's unexpected but makes sense with what Cypress Corners stands for."

Bree smiled. "You get it. Good. I think you and your family will love it here."

The couple left, the wife chatting excitedly as her husband nodded. They were hooked, and Bree entered their contact info into the database.

"They loved the house," Noah Brady said. "Good work."

Bree shrugged as she faced him. "Sorry if they bugged you, Noah. I didn't expect them to peek into the back office."

"No worries." He smiled. "The door was open."

"So do you and Jessie have plans this weekend?"

Noah grinned. "We have Max this weekend, so I think we'll be heading to Rick and Harmony's for their Sunday picnic."

Max was Noah's six-year-old son. He was adorable, and Jessie was as in love with him as she was with her husband.

"Ah, the picnic," Bree said with a nod.

"You haven't gone to one yet, Bree. How have you managed that?"

She winked. "I'm cagey."

"It'll come for you."

Bree shook her head. "Nope. I'm not on their matchmaking radar. By design."

Noah laughed. "You think so."

"Why?" She swallowed. "What do you know?"

Noah threw up his hands. "Nothing, I swear. Jessie has been trying to figure out who might be a match, though."

"Yeah, your wife is like that. Now that her sister is married and settled out there on the east side with Billy, she's looking for another project."

"True. She did love planning Shannon's wedding on New Year's."

"Then she can take the next few months off."

He smirked at her. "I'll be sure to tell her you said that."

It was Bree's turn to laugh. "I'll tell her myself, when I see her."

Noah gave her a two-finger wave and walked out of the model home. He looked a lot like the surfer guy he'd been before getting into construction, and he was apparently as easygoing as he was good looking. He was a great fit for her friend Jessie, who tended to overthink things. Bree had some of that going on too, but she'd taught herself to let the little things go. Not when it came to righting this model for Monday, though.

She straightened and cleaned and set everything to rights. It was picture-perfect. She frowned. How long had she struggled with that image crap? How long had she bowed to her mother's criticisms and her father's disapproval? Jeez, way too long.

She stowed her tablet and as she was about to tuck her phone in it dinged.

Call me, Sabrina.

Bree cursed softly. How did her mother do that? She never

called either. No. She summoned Bree, who had to jump at the
bell.

Certain she was every kind of sucker, she tapped on the
phone and made the call. Her mother answered on the first ring.

"Hello, Sabrina."

"Hi, Mom. What's up?"

Her mother sniffed. "Up? Why, nothing dear. Everything is
where it always is."

Bree rolled her eyes. "All right. How is everything?"

"Everything is well, Sabrina. Your father's dinner is next
week."

Bree's stomach clenched. "Oh?"

The clicking of her mother's tongue echoed across the
miles from Cypress Corners to Heathrow. "It's always on May
first. You know this."

"Yes, I do. Sorry." She winced. Why was she always
apologizing to her mother? "How are your plans going?"

"Your father's office has everything in hand, along with
the staff here at the house. Have you considered my
suggestion?"

Last month her mother began angling for a fix-up date to
accompany Bree to the event. Of the three men put before her,

each one had traits that put them too close to what dating her father might feel like.

"I told you I would attend, Mom. That's all I'll say on that."

"Alone? Sabrina, really." More huffing from her side of the call. "Don't tell me you're dating someone down there on the ranch?"

"The ranch?" Bree just shook her head. Every time her mother even mentioned Cypress she came up with some countryfied description. "I'm not dating anyone." That was true, technically.

"Is there no one you could bring with you? Perhaps one of the salespeople? Perhaps the director or golf pro?"

Really? Those men would be preferable to her daughter's coming alone?

"No."

"There's no one?" Her mother's voice slipped into that singsong tone that always put Bree on high alert. "You will have to be partnered for dinner, dear. Leave it to me. I'll provide your date."

Not on a bet! "Actually, I have someone in mind."

"But you just told me there was no one."

"There is, but it's very early days."

"Oh, good! The table will be even now."

"Yes, we mustn't have an uneven table."

"Sabrina, please. As long as you're bringing someone suitable...he is suitable, isn't he?"

Derek's more than suitable face and form flashed in Bree's mind. Her cheeks burned but she managed to keep her voice even.

"He's suitable, but I haven't mentioned the party to him yet."

"Don't dawdle. You're always dawdling."

Bree clenched her teeth. "Was there anything else?"

"I suppose it's too much to expect you to come for dinner on Sunday?"

"I'm busy, Mom. Sorry."

Silence. Deafening silence. "Very well. Good evening, Sabrina."

"Good bye, Mom."

The call disconnected and Bree scowled at the counter. Every time she felt like she was finally making her own way her mother provided a stark reminder that she was a failure. A screw-up. A colossal disappointment.

And now she had to attend her father's annual May Day pat-on-the-back dinner. With a date. She could ask Derek.

It could ruin what they were beginning to share. What she was beginning to learn about him and about herself.

"It could ruin everything," she whispered.

Her phone dinged again and she saw she had a text from Derek.

Dinner tonight?

She didn't even hesitate, surprising herself.

Sure. Tavern?

Sounds good. See you at 7?

7

She clutched her phone and let out a breath. She might be uncertain about asking him to her father's event, but she had absolutely no doubt about one thing.

She wanted to spend time with Derek, and she wasn't going to miss any opportunity.

Chapter 11

Derek made his way to the tavern. He'd debated over texting Bree for all of five minutes. He'd managed to resist the urge to grab her in the breakroom yesterday morning, but just barely. She'd been her usual proper professional, but he knew what was beneath those sedate clothes she wore. Yes, she had a smoking hot body. He hadn't needed to get her naked to confirm that, but the feel of her skin had been beyond his imagination. The way she'd lost herself beneath him? That was a surprise too. Her cool patrician blood ran hot.

"Derek Stone, right?" the girl at the hostess stand asked.

"Hello. Joy?" At her nod he said, "How are you?"

"Good. Bree's at the bar.

He froze his expression. "Oh?"

Joy smirked. There was no way he'd out Bree as coming here to meet him. "I'll just head in."

He stepped towards the bar in the tavern and took a long minute to just look at Bree. He'd been surprised when she'd agreed to dinner with him. This was Cypress, after all. Everyone would know they were dating unless they played this right. He was no liar, though. Deflect? Sure. Distract? Definitely. That he could do. From what he knew of Bree, she was upfront as well.

He recognized a few people in the tavern, and nodded when they saw him. Ben and Tammy Chapman sat over near the fireplace, a baby with a shock of dark hair propped in a highchair between them. Tammy waved and Derek nodded in return.

Noah and Jessie Brady were sharing a pizza with a blond little boy at a table set near the front windows. Jessie called Derek's name and gave him an enthusiastic wave which he returned with a more subdued one of his own.

It was weird, but he never really connected with any of the people he worked with at Chapman. He never joined the other clerks for pickup basketball games or to grab a movie and beer. Eli was the closest thing he had to a friend, and even their relationship wasn't very deep.

He joined her at the bar. "Hey, Bree."

She swiveled on her seat, flicking her hair over one shoulder. "Hey there, Derek."

He bit back a smile. "Great minds think alike."

She laughed a little. "Apparently."

He sat on the barstool next to her, leaning his elbows on the bar. "We're in the fishbowl. Just so you know."

"Yeah, I thought that might happen."

Her voice sounded a little flat, and he angled closer to her.

"Are you all right?"

Her eyes were wide on him, and then she waved a hand. "I'm fine. Just dealing with some family stuff."

His face was close to hers and he breathed her in. She seemed to want quiet and, since he had no idea how to start a conversation about "family stuff," he made the conscious decision to follow her lead. He was used to hiding all of his family shit. This wouldn't be a big deal.

"How do you want to play this?" he asked her.

She licked her lips. "How about we go to Joy and ask for a table?"

Derek glanced over at the hostess stand and saw that Bree's friend wasn't going to fall for it. "She's not going to buy it."

"She's not the one I'm concerned with."

He followed Bree's gaze to the dining area. Yes, there were a lot of eyes out there. "We're coworkers, Bree. You're helping me with my home purchase."

She leaned away from him, as if she remembered to maintain some distance in public. He didn't care for himself. He'd hidden a lot of things in his life but dating Bree wouldn't even show up on that list. This was her town, though. Her fishbowl.

A small smile curved her lips and he was seized with the urge to kiss her. Clearing his throat, he walked over to the hostess stand.

"Joy, do you think you could find a table for Bree and me? We decided to grab a bite together."

Joy raised a brow and then grinned. "Already done." She took up two menus and breezed past him, her nose in the air.

Chuckling, he followed her and waved for Bree to join them. He and Bree were soon seated not far from Noah and Jessie.

"Hello there, Derek," Jessie said. "Have you met our son, Max?"

Derek knew that Noah and Jessie had only been together for about a year, but it was clear from the bright smile on the little boy's face that he loved the way Jessie introduced him.

"Nice to meet you, Max," Derek said with a nod. "Hi, Noah."

"Hi, Derek." His eyes shifted to Bree. "Bree."

Bree's cheeks were a little pink but she maintained that smooth exterior. "Hi, guys."

"Having dinner together?" Jessie asked, her eyes

twinkling.

Bree clicked her tongue as she took her seat. "Never mind, Pixie."

Jessie laughed out loud and Noah chuckled. Derek sat across from Bree and put the other couple out of his mind. Drinks and dinner ordered, beer and burger for him, white wine and salmon for her, they still sat in relative silence. Her brows were drawn together and every so often she looked like she was going to say something to him and then pressed her lips together.

"Are you sure you're all right?" he asked as their meal was nearly finished.

Bree sat back, folding her hands in her lap. "I have something to ask you and you can totally say no."

Derek smiled, and thought to tease her a little. The urge surprised him. He wasn't exactly the charming teaser his friend Eli was.

"Bree, I can't think of anything you could ask me that I would say no to."

Her eyes flared and she shook her head. "Stop that. Seriously, I have this thing I have to go to on the first."

"Of May?"

She nodded. "My father hosts this May Day party every

year. I've been summoned."

"What kind of party is it?"

"Oh, the usual. Look how well we're doing! Look how beautiful my wife is! Look how perfect my daughter is! The usual."

"Sounds painful."

"Oh, the food is fantastic and the drinks poured freely. The pressure and guilt? Yeah, that sucks for me."

"So don't go."

She gaped at him. "There is no way I can avoid this. I moved to Cypress to get out of that cage, but I have to check in periodically with my parole officer."

He laughed softly. "You paint quite a picture. It's no big surprise you're so good at sales."

That got him the smile he was after. "So will you come? I can introduce you as anything you like?"

"Anything?"

"Within reason."

"I'll pick date. Seems innocuous."

"Good." Her hand covered his. "Thank you."

"We can kill two birds with one stone, I'm thinking."

She tilted her head. "What birds would those be?"

"I'll be closing on my house just a couple of days before. Why don't we turn the painful party into our own celebration?"

"You're serious."

"Haven't you heard what they say about me? I'm always serious."

"That's not exactly true."

His body tightened. "No. Not exactly. And not always."

She glanced to her right and he followed her line of vision. Noah's little family was gone, but Tammy Chapman was on her way over.

"Well, hello," Tammy said.

The leggy brunette wore a grin as she shifted the chubby baby in her arms. "Look, Raffaella. It's our friends Bree and Derek."

The baby blinked at Derek and he was caught by its serious expression. "Raffaella," he said in greeting.

Ben joined them, shaking droplets of water off his head. "Hey, guys. I pulled the car up front."

"Is it raining?" Bree asked.

"Cats and dogs," Ben said.

Tammy pulled a soft-looking blanket seemingly out of nowhere and covered the baby's dark curls. "Come on, sweetheart. Daddy brought the chariot around." She looked meaningfully at Bree, but Bree wasn't giving anything away. "Good night, friends."

"Good night," Bree said.

Derek nodded to Ben and Tammy and they finally left the table. He looked back at Bree. "Damn, you're good."

"Years of practice."

She sounded a little sad, and he found himself wanting to bring out another smile. A smile and maybe something more. A sigh. A scream.

"How do you want to play this now?" he asked.

She drew her cell phone out of her bag and made a show of checking her messages. Her body language said she wasn't really paying him much attention, but that was only if someone didn't know her body like he did. Like he wanted to know even more.

"The Sales Center is closed tomorrow," she said as if to herself.

"It is."

She put her phone on the table with a loud sigh. "I'd love to get away for the weekend."

He caught on to what she was saying, or he certainly hoped

so. "How about at a charming inn set near the lakeshore?"

She breathed in, and her entire body seemed to shiver slightly. "Sounds just perfect."

He took out his phone, to further cement the image that they weren't on a date. Looking down, he texted her his room number. She lifted her phone when it dinged, smiling down at the screen.

She eyed him with a smile. "Seems I have plans now."

"Good." He took the check from their server when it came, waving her hand away. "You get the next one. You never know when we'll run into each other again."

Standing, she pulled a jacket out of her bag. It was a sporty little thing, and when she settled the hood on her head she looked adorable and hot. "See you later, Derek."

***

Bree kept the smile from her face as she exited the tavern. Joy gave her a smug expression.

"Good night, Joy."

She grinned. "I bet it will be."

She walked to her car, the rain drops tapping on her hood as she made her way. She willed her heartrate to slow. She was going to Derek's room at the inn tonight. For the whole night, if she could admit that to herself. A clandestine assignation, or something out of a PBS drama like that.

All of this cloak-and-dagger stuff really wasn't her style, and it didn't seem to be Derek's either. Still, he'd played along with her charade there at the tavern. Jessie had looked like she wasn't fooled. Tammy either, for that matter. Their respective guys had been clueless, but weren't guys always the last to know?

Now, Joy. That girl knew what was up. Bree didn't worry that she would say anything, though. She wasn't a little Lettie, after all. Her mother, on the other hand? Mrs. Rollins might look like a mother hen but she was as sharp-eyed as the Sandhill cranes that walked all over Cypress. Bree worried about her cover story when she would inevitably run into the innkeeper, but then shrugged it off. She wasn't a teen sneaking out for kicks anymore. Not that she'd managed to pull that little trick very often back in the day.

Her car door creaked as she opened it, reminding her that she should get Claire Chapman's dad to take another look at it. The guy was a wizard with old cars, and her grandmother's baby needed special care. Pushing her hood from her head, she started the engine and headed home. She'd about had it with her work outfit today, and if she was going to try something new she was going to wear something new. Or at least, almost new. Different, anyway.

It was still raining pretty hard as she changed into jeans and a stretchy pink knit top. The moisture had put a wave in her hair she wasn't too fond of, but she just brushed it out and let it fall. Going through her drawers, she chose what to bring for tonight.

She'd seen his face when he spotted her lacy underwear, so she picked out a couple of sets to put in her favorite tote bag. The little whales swimming all over it eyed her with grins. She added a ribbed long-sleeve T, speckled pajama pants and a pair of fluffy socks too, although she wasn't sure if Derek was a PJs kind of guy. A flush washed over her as she recalled just how fine he'd looked in just those boxer briefs. Throwing in a zippered bag with her toothbrush and toiletries, she was ready to go. Shouldering the bag, she hurried downstairs.

Remembering the white wine chilling in the fridge, she slipped that into her tote bag too. Growing up, her mother had instilled upon her the importance of always being prepared. She certainly hadn't meant preparing for an extended booty-call, but this would simply be yet another thing Margaret James wouldn't know about.

Her car's tires hissed on the rain-slick road as she made her way to the inn. There was ample parking, which she considered a good sign. That would mean most of the guests were still out and about. Her luck held as she passed through the lobby and up the grand staircase to the guest rooms. Breathing a sigh of relief, she found Derek's room and knocked on the door. He opened it, and suddenly she could hardly breathe at all.

He'd changed too, and now wore jeans that hung just right off of his narrow hips. A dark green Henley, she just loved a Henley, stretched across his broad shoulders and outlined every taut muscle in his chest. He was barefoot, which she found sexy for some reason.

His dark eyes were intense, as they usually were. His sculpted lips were set but his posture was rigid. A smile pulled at his lips and he seemed to relax a little.

"Bree."

Oh, the way he said her name. Straightening her shoulders, she smiled. "Are you going to invite me in?"

He stepped back and she was in the clear. She must have shown something on her face, because he chuckled. "What?"

"You look like you're on the run," he said.

She laughed lightly. "I am. From the prying eyes of Mrs. Rollins."

"She's a nosy lady, but she seems to keep out of the guests' business."

Bree tossed her bag on the nearest chair. "I really don't care about myself. I just didn't want to drag you into some sort of drama."

"No worries. I'm a big boy."

"Yeah, you are."

He kissed her, a soft kiss that seemed to wrap itself around her. "I'm just glad you're here."

She looked around his guest room. Ambient lighting, high-end furnishings, muted colors. If she didn't know better she might think she was standing in a five-star luxury hotel room. "Wow, this is really nice."

"It is." He took off her rain jacket and set it on the chair beside her bag. "You've never stayed here?"

She shook her head. "I've been to events here, but they were held downstairs or out on the terrace."

"The downstairs is nice but it's a little too old-fashioned for my tastes."

"Yes, Mrs. Rollins likes that Old Florida Victorian vibe.

Pastels, rattan, potted plants."

He nodded. "Would you like a drink?"

Smiling, she withdrew the wine bottle from her bag. "Sure."

He returned the expression and took the bottle. Pouring the wine into two crystal glasses from the sideboard, he handed her one and clinked it with his. "To getting away for the weekend."

She sipped the cool crisp wine and felt the worries of the week melt away. The call from her mother. It was like there was nothing but tonight, and she was on board with that.

"Thanks again for agreeing to come to my father's party."

"I've been to enough of those society things to know what to expect." He took her glass and set it back down with his. "I don't want to talk about family stuff, Bree. Do you?"

Slowly, she shook her head. "Nope."

He drew her closer. "Good. Because I've been wondering about something ever since you took off that cute little jacket."

Her pulse tripped again and she put on an expression of innocence. "What's that?"

He stroked a finger over her neck and slipped it just under the collar of her top. "What color underwear are you wearing tonight?"

"Oh?" Pleasing tingles spread over her from his fingertip. "You didn't do your due diligence?"

He stroked ever so gently beneath her bra strap. "Not yet, I'm afraid."

"I'll make it easy on you." Pulling away from his touch, she reached down and pulled her shirt up and over her head. "Violet."

His eyes ran over her breasts and her nipples pulled tight. "Not easy at all, Bree."

Her gaze dropped to the front of his jeans. No. He was clearly hard and it was because of her. Once again, that strength she'd felt with him the other night came over her.

"Lose the shirt, counselor."

He did as she ordered and she stared at him. "You're beautiful, Derek. Do you know that?"

"Beautiful? If you say so."

She stepped closer to him. "Trust me on this."

He stilled for a beat, and then his mouth was on hers again. This wasn't soft and slow, like his earlier kiss. No. It was hot and hungry and just what she needed.

The smooth cotton coverlet was cool beneath her skin as he stripped off the rest of her clothes. His body was hot in contrast, and her breasts ached from his hair-roughened skin against her.

"God, I have to get inside you." His mouth was everywhere. On her breasts, her belly, her center. "Tell me I can."

"Yes." She ran her fingers through his hair, tugging as she drew him back up to her. "Yes, Derek."

He sucked in a breath as she stroked him. He was naked now too, although she didn't get to see that particular show. No, she'd been lost in his touch, his kisses, as he'd apparently stripped. She thought she might have to get him to do that again sometime, but then her mind went blank to everything but what he was doing to her now.

He licked her, slowly and deliberately, and then came up on his knees. They were in the center of his king-size bed, and she was splayed beneath him. As he reached beneath the plump pillows beside her and withdrew a foil packet, her body flushed hotter still. It had been so long since she'd slept with a guy. There hadn't been anyone since she'd moved to Cypress. This guy, though? Oh, he was so worth breaking her losing streak.

"That's it, baby." He shifted again, bringing that ridged belly up against her. He kissed her, rubbing his cock over her until she thought she'd die from the tension.

163

"Derek, please."

He lost some of that control that always seemed to cling to him. His fingers shook a little as he tore open the condom wrapper and took care of it. And then he moved right to where she needed him most. He was huge. Hard and so perfect she cried out.

He stilled. "Bree, are you okay?"

"Take me, Derek." She moved, loving how he filled her. "Oh, please."

He slid further inside, stretching her in the best way as he began to move. They found their rhythm, and she held on to his braced arms as he rode her. Their breathing was labored and sweat broke out on her brow as she gave into the most amazing time she'd ever had with a guy.

"Sweet, Bree." He bent down and gave her a quick kiss. "You're so sweet."

She broke in the next second, her orgasm pulling every muscle taut as she cried out again. He continued to move, driving her closer to another release as he continued to murmur incoherent words of obvious pleasure. With a cry of his own, he came.

After, he held her close as their bodies seemed to fit

perfectly against each other's.

"Christ," he said again. "That was fucking amazing."

She managed a small laugh at the profanity. "Yeah, it was."

He got up and she finally got that show she'd craved earlier. He returned from the bathroom and retrieved their glasses of wine.

Taking a cleansing breath, she sat up and took the glass from him. "Still cold."

"Mostly."

She looked at this guy, who appeared pretty darn proud of himself right now, and felt a lightness she hadn't felt in years.

She might not know what this was between her and Derek but she loved that she could be herself with him. It was a first for her, and she wasn't going to waste it.

Chapter 12

"Isn't this so much better than the fishbowl?"

Bree made a sound of agreement and cuddled closer against Derek's chest. Fragrant steam rose from the bubbly water in the tub, making his muscles relax more than they had in recent memory. Her round little ass was up against his groin, but his dick was only mildly interested at the moment. They'd had two bouts already, and he and his dick were content for now.

He brought his lips to her shoulder and dropped a kiss on her dewy skin. They were putting the big bathtub in his guest room to good use tonight. After having the single best fuck of his life in his bed, he hadn't though they could improve on it. He was quickly proven wrong when they'd splashed and sloshed in the tub a while later. Now they were still wrapped in each other and he wasn't seized with the usual urge to get her the hell out of his room. Not like his apartment in Boston, anyway. He couldn't get a woman out of there fast enough.

"So what are the plans for this weekend?" she asked, her voice thick and drowsy.

"Whatever you want." He stroked his hands over her arms, finding her skin slick from the soapy water. "We can just stay here."

She looked at him over one creamy shoulder. "Keep me your dirty little secret?"

He caught her smile. "My clean little secret, but sure. If you want me to."

She sighed and faced forward again. "I don't know what I want, but this has been amazing so far."

"I have no idea what time it is, but I'd guess we haven't even been here for two hours."

She took his hand in hers, threading their fingers together. "This is new for me, you know. Letting go with a guy."

His mind went back to their time in his bed. Hell, their time right here in the tub. "Glad to be your first in that respect. Your letting go is pretty amazing."

She wriggled closer and his body woke up a little more. Tracing a finger over his palm, she touched on his scars. "I noticed these before, Derek."

"What?" Like he didn't know.

"These scars. What are they from?"

He resisted the urge to pull his hand away from her. Instead, he opened his palm to her touch. "They're rope burns."

She turned slightly toward him, causing water to slosh around them. "Rope burns? How would a lawyer get rope burns." She winked. "Wait. You're not into anything kinky, are you?"

He laughed, and the tightness in his chest eased a little. "No. I got these when I was a kid."

She faced him now, running her hand over his shoulders. "How did you get them?"

He pressed his lips together, and then cursed softly. "I got them from my father."

Her mind worked, and he saw when she came to the conclusion. Part of it, anyway. "You're always slipping nautical terms into conversation. You did this on a boat."

"Yes. I was sailing with my father." The familiar bitterness rose up but he swallowed it back down. "He was trying to teach me, although he only did it to show up my mother's brother."

"Your mother's brother?"

"My Uncle Jackson. He took me sailing every weekend until the summer I turned eight. Then Eddie decided it didn't look right if he pawned his son off on his brother-in-law."

She kept stroking him, his arms, his thigh, almost as if she didn't realize she was doing it. He took the comfort she gave him, though. He'd never told anyone this story, but the mood and the girl made his tongue loose.

"My father pushed me really hard. It was raining, and the rope was biting into my hands but he wouldn't let me stop until I executed every maneuver and knot correctly."

She took his hand again, looking at the tiny scars closely. "You blistered, I bet."

"Like a bitch. My mother tried to take care of my hands afterwards but Eddie wouldn't let her. He told her not to treat me like a pussy."

Bree gasped. "That's harsh."

"Yes, well Eddie's a son-of-a-bitch. The next day she treated my hands, but the blisters had formed and split and formed over and over again." He shrugged, and gently pulled his hand from hers. "I healed."

"Your hands, anyway."

"No one could see them after a while. In college I rowed crew, so I had callouses." He cupped her face and brought his brow to hers. "I don't want to talk about this anymore."

She lifted herself and straddled his waist. "You don't have to." Kissing him, she sighed. "Thank you for telling me."

He moved beneath her, grabbing her ass with both hands. "If anybody asks, I'll swear you used water torture on me."

She threw her head back and laughed, the sound bright and

just right to send the rest of that hateful memory from his mind.

Later, after making more splashes in the big tub, they each threw on some clothes. He wore sweats and one of a dozen BC T-shirts he owned and she wore spotted pants and a thin shirt. The fuzzy socks on her feet just added to the surprisingly sexy outfit. They snuggled together in the seating area and ate from the minibar.

"Those pajamas are adorable," he teased as he popped another Macadamia nut into his mouth.

She crossed her arms, no doubt unaware that he could see the outline of her nipples in her thin shirt. "And what do you wear to bed, counselor?"

He spread his arms wide. "You're looking at it."

"So you went to Boston College."

"I did. Undergrad, and then Harvard law."

"Impressive."

He shrugged it off. "You?"

"College? Florida State."

"You're not a Gator?"

She wrinkled her nose and took some nuts from the can. "Nope."

He lifted his chin towards the remote for the entertainment

system set on the wide leather ottoman in front of them. "Do you want to watch a movie or something?"

"Sure." She grabbed the remote and came closer, fitting up against his side like she'd always been there. "We could use the time to build up your strength."

He rolled his eyes. "Baby, don't you worry about me."

She laughed and flicked through the channels until they found a romcom. It was mindless entertainment, and as they watched the couple on the screen fall inevitably in love he realized she wasn't the only one with a first tonight.

He'd never done any of this before. The bedroom workout, sure. But the bath. The talk. The kidding around. This was all new territory for him. They might both be keeping all of this a secret for now, but how long could that last?

At the moment, he couldn't care less. Bree was here now. She was in his arms and in his bed. If she was in his thoughts afterwards, what harm could there be?

It wasn't like they were falling in love.

***

Bree awoke on Saturday morning, all wrapped up in Derek's long limbs. She hadn't spent the night with a guy in…ever, really. The sheets were Egyptian cotton, and silky-

171

smooth against her skin. She'd tugged her pajamas back on after
their last roll-around, but Derek had only put on his briefs. Right
now her top was pushed up almost to her neck. Derek's hands,
those big strong hands of his, stroked over her belly as she
turned to face him.

"Early riser?" she asked, slowly stretching as she opened
her eyes.

He flashed a smile, one of those wide smiles he didn't
show very often. "Do you want me to answer that?"

She caught his meaning and laughed. "Derek Stone, the
man of the morning charm."

His brow furrowed. "That's a new one on me."

He settled back on the many pillows and she turned to face
him. He looked really good despite the mussed hair and
shadowed jaw, or maybe because of it.

Unable to resist, she placed a hand on his chest. He was
warm and strong and she could feel his heartbeat beneath her
palm. "What time is it?"

Grabbing his phone off of the nightstand, he tapped the
screen. "Almost eight thirty."

She murmured and sank down on his chest. "That's nice."

He rubbed a hand down her back and then smacked her

butt. "I ordered in breakfast."

That made her pop open her eyes. "I didn't know Mrs. Rollins offered that."

"She does. She even told me she would include her famous cinnamon rolls."

Bree sat up now. "Okay, you've got me."

"Do I, now?"

She took a good look at him now. The words seemed offhand but the expression on his face was shuttered. Here was the cool Derek she'd known from the first. She would play it like him, then.

"For cinnamon rolls? There's little I wouldn't do."

She seemed to crack his mask a little. "Seems to me there was little you wouldn't do just last night."

Her entire body flushed hot. "Stop that."

He shrugged. "Just turning on my, what did you call it? Morning charm?"

She pushed herself out of the bed. "Never mind. I'm going to hop in the shower if that's okay."

"Sure. Breakfast should be here in a couple of minutes."

She went into the ridiculously-luxurious bathroom and took a quick shower under its six showerheads. Wrapping a towel around herself, she twisted her hair over her shoulder and peeked out into the guest room. Derek wore his sweats and T-shirt once more, and mussed casual Derek was pretty darn eye-catching. She heard a knock at the door and ducked back into the bathroom.

As she dressed she heard the muffled sounds of Derek's half of the conversation. If she had to pick out the identity of the person who delivered their breakfast, she would guess it was Joy. She blew out a breath. So much for hiding out in anonymity.

Slipping on her underwear, today's would be blue, she chose jeans and a scooped-neck T in sunny yellow. She towel-dried her hair as she joined him. The scent of freshly-brewed coffee and those heavenly cinnamon rolls filled the room.

"Mmm, yes," she said.

His head turned and he flashed her a smile. "Heard that last night too, if I recall correctly."

"Counselor, I seriously doubt you ever recall anything incorrectly."

He dipped his head. "And now you've got me."

"Turned my words on me, did you?" She wrinkled her nose at him. "I'll give you that, Due Diligence."

Shaking his head, he lifted the metal covers on their breakfasts. "Today's Belgian waffle day, apparently."

Their plates were piled with two thick waffles each, smothered in at least four types of fruit and clouds of whipped cream. She poured them each a cup of coffee and sat across from him. "Looks like we have our work cut out for us."

"No joke." He took a drink of his coffee and set his cup down. "I say we save the rolls for later."

"Later?"

He blinked at her as he regarded her. "We have the whole weekend, Bree. Don't we?"

"We do." She took a bit of fluffy waffle, rolling her eyes in delight. "So good."

He made a sound of happy agreement. "And brought by your friend Joy."

Bree wiped her mouth on a linen napkin. "I thought that was her voice."

"Is that a problem?"

"Not for me. Like you said before, it's not like we're having an affair."

He gave a sage nod. "True. But keeping this a secret just grew exponentially more difficult."

175

She thought for a long minute. "Derek, I don't care if people know we're involved. I just don't want them to jump to conclusions."

"What kinds of conclusions?"

"Please. Have you taken a look around Cypress Corners? Couples and families and babies. The fishbowl runneth over."

He laughed at her turn of phrase. "I'm sure there are people seeing other people around here, too. Not everybody gets, what did you call it? Caught in the net?"

"I suppose." She picked up a perfect strawberry and dragged it through the whipped cream. "I just don't want you to regret this."

As she took a bit of the berry, his eyes darkened. "Baby, I doubt I'll regret anything that involves you and me."

On that sensually-charged note, they continued to eat their breakfast in relative silence. Her mind worked, though. Over everything they'd shared last night, of course. But also over what they'd done just this morning.

His words were almost sweet, and warmer than she might have expected from him just last week. He'd told her that awful story about his father last night. His mask had been nowhere in sight as he related what had to be such a traumatic memory. It was hard to imagine this self-assured strong man as a vulnerable little boy but she'd heard it in his tone. His father had really screwed him up, or certainly tried to.

Her father might be a pompous ass but he wasn't cruel. No. Arthur James was self-involved and all about image but aside from dismissals he didn't really push Bree beyond his expectations of the perfect daughter. Since she'd failed on that count, she supposed was off the hook. Relatively speaking, anyway. There was still that party to attend on the first.

After a while he set his empty plate aside. "What do you want to do today?"

Pushing her remaining waffle toward him, she drank more of her coffee. "Since your closing is next Thursday, did you want to go pick out some furniture?"

His face brightened. "You would help me with that?"

"Sure." She beamed a smile at him. "I love shopping."

"I don't, but there's a lot of space to fill."

"What did you place in Boston look like?"

"A lot like this room, actually."

"So not very homey."

He chuckled. "No, I guess not."

"Never fear. I might not have Jessie's knack for staging but

177

I can certainly help you pick out what you might need. I'm thinking we head east to Melbourne."

"Why?"

"Because Melbourne has tons of furniture stores." She winked. "And the Atlantic Ocean, of course."

He smiled. "You know just what to say to me, don't you?"

She crossed her arms. "Maybe."

He leaned over the table and kissed her, quick and sweeter than the berries and cream. She might not know what this was, but she would enjoy it. Live in the moment, for once in her life.

Neither of them had any other commitments. They were both going into this thing with their eyes wide open. It would be incredible while it lasted.

And after? Bree just wouldn't think about that.

Chapter 13

Derek sat at his desk on Monday morning, thumbing through his emails. It had taken him two cups of coffee to get his head in the game today, since he'd spent the entire weekend with Bree. They'd managed to order all of the furniture he would need to outfit his new house, and on Sunday they drove around Cypress getting ideas for what color to paint the exterior. In the end they'd settled on a gray-blue that would really give the house a New England feel.

He looked over a couple of contracts that came in late on Friday afternoon, along with some memos regarding other improvements on the property. It wouldn't be long before the Active Adult community would take up a big part of his day's work. He thought about all the furniture he'd picked out with Bree and wondered if she would come help his mother arrange her new house once it was built and ready for occupancy.

Someone knocked on the door and he looked up to see a guy he didn't know standing there. He was broad but soft in the middle, and wore a Florida State shirt.

"Derek Stone?" he asked, brushing his thinning hair back from his face.

"Yes," Derek answered in a tone that should put the guy on

notice. Clearly he was Derek Stone. This was his office, after all.

"I wanted to see you about your application."

Derek thought for a second before it hit him. "My house color. Yes, I sent that to the design committee this morning."

The guy smiled. "That's me. I'm the chair." He stuck out a hand. "Johnny Knox."

Derek shook his hand. He recognized the name. It was on a number of memos stating that the committee was taking a very long time to approve some residents' improvement applications. Noah and Rick didn't have anything nice to say about him, either. Unless Derek was mistaken, the term blowhard was often used.

"What is this visit about, Johnny?"

The guy sat without asking. "I wondered if the color you chose is suitable for your house."

"I chose it, so it's suitable."

Johnny nodded. "I'm not a big fan of blue."

"Then it's good you won't be living in my house."

"But the front door."

"What about it? I chose a color a shade darker than the faded paint color on it now."

"Red."

"Yes, red."

Johnny blinked at Derek's tone. Good.

"I suppose it will work then."

"Thank you. While you're here, I have a few questions for you." Derek turned to his laptop and pulled up a few pending applications. "Is there a reason you're dragging your feet on these applications?"

Johnny blustered. "Dragging my feet?"

"These aren't ridiculous color choices, Johnny. The fences applied for fit within their allowable lot lines."

"Still, people can't expect to get their answers right away."

"Why not?"

Johnny's mouth dropped open. "There is a procedure."

Derek nodded. "Which these residents have adhered to. I'm the in-house counsel here now, Johnny. I have a lot of items to review for Cypress. Contracts. Proposals. Other committee business. Deciding what color a resident chooses to paint their front door? Not a high priority in my book."

"I suppose."

"Get these reviews approved as swiftly as you can. If there is a problem, maybe we should revisit the application process."

The threat was there. To dismantle the committee that this

guy clearly thought was his exalted office. His cheeks were red as he nodded.

"The committee will review what we have in-house, if that works for you."

"It does."

Johnny came to his feet. "I just want to make sure that Cypress Corners continues to present the image we've all strived so hard to project."

"With Mr. Forbes and the Cypress Institute involved, that's not a concern." He paused a beat. "Certainly not solely a concern of yours."

Johnny's head bobbed. "Very well. Thank you, Mr. Stone."

Derek gave a curt nod and the guy left his office. "He is a blowhard."

"You sound like Noah."

Derek looked over at his still-open door to see Jessie grinning at him. "Hey, Jessie."

The pretty Pixie stepped into his office. "Although sometimes he uses more colorful words."

"I wouldn't waste any more words on him." Derek found a smile. "And I'm a lawyer. We love our words."

She nodded. "So you had dinner with Bree on Friday night."

Derek kept his expression even at the swift turn of topic. "Yes I did."

"I didn't hear much from her this weekend."

"Are you trying to ask me something, Jessie?"

She fiddled with the buttons on her sweater for a few seconds. "Oh, no. I was just making conversation."

"Sure you were," Bree said from the hallway.

Jessie jumped, then smiled in Bree's direction. "Hi, Bree."

"Hi, Jessie."

"Um, did you want to talk to Derek?" Jessie winked. "You know. Talk?"

"Pixie, please," Bree said with a laugh.

Jessie grinned and waved before rushing off. Bree looked at Derek, her brow knit. "Problem?"

"Not now." He was being completely honest. The crap with Johnny as well as anything else he'd reviewed this morning left his mind when she smiled at him.

She closed the door and came closer. "We're all set for the closing next week."

"Thanks." He stood and came around his desk to kiss her.

"This feels a little clandestine, Bree."

"I think it's a little like closing the barn door once the horse has gotten out, or some other folksy comment."

"Cat out of the bag?"

"Maybe." Her eyes sparkled up at him. "Fish out of the bowl?"

"That's not good for the fish."

She reached up to place her hands behind his neck. "Just kiss me. We can worry about the rest of it later."

He brought his mouth to hers and she parted her lips. Kissing her deeply, he relished the taste of her. Sun and sweetness and Bree. Pulling back, he pressed his brow to hers. "What about lunch today?"

She shook her head. "Can't, I'm afraid. I have to take a tour out on the east side of the property."

He gave a dramatic shiver. "With the gators and wild boar?"

"Not exactly." She bit her bottom lip and then smiled. "We're touring the Active Adult site."

"Finally."

"I thought your mother was moving in with you."

"Yes, but that's not something I want indefinitely."

She kissed him again, lightly this time. "It'll cramp your style, I bet."

"I don't know about that. I just want to see her safe and settled."

He saw the question in her eyes. She already knew his father had abused him. How long before she figured out that his mother was a victim a lot more often?

She stepped out of his arms and back towards the door. "I'd better go. Rick and Eli are leading the charge today."

"I'm sure I'll be briefed on it."

Before she opened the door, she threw him one more smile. "I am free for dinner, though."

Warmth blossomed in his chest. "Done."

***

Bree tried to keep her head in the game as the cart made it's bumpy way over towards the east side of the property. Most of the sales staff were present, except for Oliver. He was holding down the fort this afternoon. Mondays were usually very busy, and from this morning's traffic out at the model home she figured that the afternoon would probably continue the trend.

The farmhouse where Jessie's sister and her husband lived was out this way, as was the little tent-cabin near the far

185

lakeshore. Jessie had lived out there before getting together with Noah, which still gave Bree the heebie-jeebies when she thought about it. She was so not an outdoorsy kind of girl. No, her idea of roughing it was a limited room service menu. That thought brought back everything she and Derek had shared in his very nice room at the inn.

They'd snuck down without Mrs. Rollins catching on and spent their day out in Melbourne. His house would be beautifully outfitted when he closed next week. They'd eaten out on the Intracoastal Waterway after shopping, and it had been bliss to be out of the Cypress fishbowl. They'd spent Saturday night together too, and on Sunday drove back out to the east coast for brunch. He'd taken her out on the lake in one of the small sailboats for rent at the main lakeshore in Cypress. As he'd maneuvered the little boat, she'd thought how utterly perfect he'd looked. She wouldn't think about that horrid story about his father. It was clear he still loved the water, so the man hadn't ruined that for his son.

Nothing was said of just where they were together but it was early days. She wasn't even sure what she wanted them to be, since this was all so new for her.

Derek had looked so good when she'd rescued him from

Jessie's interrogation today, too. Yummy, even. Ready for his work week, she'd wanted to strip off his pressed clothes and roll around with him on his desk. That behavior would so not do. Thinking about it, though? She couldn't find anything wrong with that.

As Eli went on about some of the features and where, precisely, they would be located she took notes on her tablet. They would have another meeting about this. Soon, unless she missed her guess. The underground infrastructure was nearly complete, and paving of roads would soon be underway. In her mind's eye she could see the neighborhood and knew it would fit in nicely with the surrounding wilder areas.

First up would be the recreation center, tennis courts etc. The golf course wasn't far, but there would be a new swim center with east side access. A full activities center and other amenities will make the fifty-five plus community very desirable. Derek would be able to rest easy with his mother living here. Separate but close by, which should be perfect. He hadn't said so, but if a man could abuse his little boy like Derek's father did, his mother must have had a horrific time of it as well.

"She'll love it here," she murmured.

"What's that, Bree?" Jessie asked from her seat beside her in the cart.

"I'm just thinking that people are going to love this."

"It's going to go like gangbusters," Eli threw in. "From the launch."

"Do we have a date on that yet?" Tammy asked.

"No," Rick answered. "I'll get with Mr. Forbes and we'll come up with a concrete date for the announcement and pertinent dates to follow."

"I bet they'll have our in-house counsel look it over," Jessie stage-whispered toward Bree.

Tammy laughed low in her throat. "I hear he's very thorough."

Bree brushed a hand over her shoulder, her nose in the air. "Hmm. Something's buzzing in my ear."

Jessie and Tammy both laughed.

"Good thing Ollie's not here," Jessie said.

Bree silently agreed with that. Ollie rivaled Lettie with his affinity for gossip.

By the time they returned to the Sales Center, tours took up the rest of her day. She hadn't solidified her dinner plans with Derek, but that hadn't stopped her from checking her phone a hundred times.

"What are you looking for?" Ollie asked.

She jumped at the sound of his voice. When the guy wasn't talking he could sneak up on someone like a Ninja.

"Never mind." Bree set her phone back down. "What are you and Todd up to tonight?"

Ollie rolled his eyes. "Inventory."

She eyed him. "You're going to help him at the store?"

"It's what you do when you're in a relationship, buttercup. Support and all of that."

"It doesn't sound like you're too put out."

"I'm not. We'll have a working dinner." He eyed her, one hand on his hip. "You can join us, you know. If you're on your own tonight?"

Bree slowly shook her head. "Interesting approach, Ollie. I'll give you props."

He stomped his foot, looking like a ticked off cherub. "Can't blame me for trying. You're keeping something secret. Some*one* secret and I can just about guess who it is."

"Just about." Bree stared him down. "Have a nice night."

He threw up his hands. "Fine. See you tomorrow."

He was smiling when he left, though. She clicked through

her laptop, sending her updated schedule to her tablet before shutting it down. Jessie bopped into the room to grab her stuff, holding her bag in front of her as she shot Bree a meaningful look.

"What?" Bree asked, keeping her voice even.

"Do you two want to join Noah and me for dinner?"

Bree's mouth dropped open. "I... I don't know who... What?"

"We're going to the tavern, Bree. Should we grab a table for four?"

"Yes," Derek said from the hallway.

Bree shot him a look, arching a brow at him. He gave her a small smile but it was the connection in those dark brown eyes that made a different kind of warmth wash over her. Something more than the sensual heat that always seemed to simmer between them.

"Sounds good," she said to Jessie, her gaze still on Derek.

Jessie let out a happy little yelp and hurried out of the salespeople's area.

"You're sure?" she asked Derek when they were alone.

He shrugged. "It's dinner, Bree. I, for one, want to spend the evening with you."

She placed a hand over her chest and inhaled deeply. "Me, too."

He waved a hand. "Then, let's go."

Bree grabbed her things and she and Derek made their way to the tavern. He walked beside her, close enough that she could all but feel him against her.

"Well, look at that pretty picture," Lettie said from beneath her crepe myrtle. "Don't you two look just lovely together."

Bree wished she could brush a hand over her shoulder like she had on the tour earlier, but this was Lettie. There was no fooling her.

"We're having dinner together, Lettie."

"Actually," Derek cut in, "I'm taking her to dinner."

Lettie's eyes sparkled. "As it should be, my dear boy."

"Have a nice night," Bree said.

"I don't have to wish the two of you the same." Lettie winked. "But I will."

Bree studied the sidewalk as Derek chuckled softly beside her.

"We're officially outed," he said, his lips close to her ear. "Are you okay with that?"

She turned her head, meeting his gaze directly. "Very."

Chapter 14

Derek directed the moving men on where to place his new furniture. The closing yesterday had gone as smoothly as silk, and now he stood in his own house. His first house, actually.

Mr. Forbes had insisted he take the rest of the afternoon off to get his house in order, and Derek had taken him up on the offer. It would be a great way to start his weekend, anyway.

Bree had been adorably flustered as the last of the paperwork came through. The seller was out-of-state, but everything was signed electronically and met with all parties' approval. He'd seen her handle several closings even in the two short weeks he'd been at Cypress, and she'd never appeared this invested. True, she stood to make a sizeable commission from the sale. He preferred to think that she was personally involved, too.

"All set, Mr. Stone," one of the moving men said.

"Let me just look everything over."

"Sure."

"There's soda in the refrigerator."

The guy looked surprised, but stocking the kitchen had been job one for Derek. He wasn't sure if he was going to actually cook a meal in the well-equipped kitchen, but he wanted to have stuff on hand should a certain gorgeous blonde spend the night.

He checked over all of the bedroom suites as they were set up, and the master and two of the guest rooms were fine. Now he looked over the big leather sectional and the dining set. It was one of those thick weathered wood tables with galvanized metal chairs pulled up to it. The chairs coordinated with the taller stools set at the high counter. A new flat screen just waited to entertain him from its spot above the fireplace.

His house had a masculine vibe, but felt fresh. That was probably due to the throw pillows and other accents that Bree had chosen for him. Lots of shades of blue and some nubby cream fabric throw that she had told him reminded her of a fisherman's sweater.

"Looks good," Derek said, signing the moving man's tablet.

"Thanks for the sodas."

The three other guys with him murmured similar sentiments and soon Derek was alone in his furnished house. Settling on the pretty awesome leather sectional, he leaned his elbows on his knees. The coffee table, a big thing made out of weathered wood, held a woven bowl with balls of thick twine.

They were monkey fists, actually. The common nautical knot didn't have any functionality in modern sailing, but it was a nice decorative element. Bree really knew his tastes then, and not just in the bedroom.

There was a pewter lantern lamp on a round side table and a poster of flags showing several common signals. She might say that Jessie was the best at house staging but the touches Bree chose made his house feel comfortable. The dark wood flooring, the light gray counters and cabinets, the oversized lighting fixtures all made him feel at home. Now he just needed to christen the thing, like a ship. Smiling at the silly reference, he texted Bree and invited her to dinner.

She answered in the affirmative so he took the new dishes he'd run through the dishwasher and rummaged in his well-stocked fridge. They could order in, of course. They'd done that a few times this week, actually. At her place, mostly. He wanted to cook for her tonight, though.

Over the past couple of days he could sense her getting nervous about the upcoming party at her parents' house. She'd repeatedly offered to let him off the hook, but he remained firm. He hoped she needed him there. If so, he would be there. This might all be new for him, but he would try to be her anchor. He chuckled at yet another nautical reference.

"Enough," he told himself.

His doorbell rang, the sound chiming throughout the house. Pulling open his front door, he found her standing there. She held a big houseplant, something dark green and shiny with touches of red, and smiled.

"Lettie's suggestion," she said from around the foliage. "It's a Red Aglaonema."

He took it from her, that and a kiss hello. "It's nice. Big."

"It's supposed to be for lovers." Bree's cheeks turned as pink as the edges of the plant's leaves. "I wasn't going to remark on the size, however."

He laughed and set the plant on the tall kitchen counter. "I don't want to think about the conversation that would have followed."

She walked around his place, tweaking and adjusting the accessories here and there. "This looks great, Derek."

"You chose everything. I really like how it all comes together."

Picking up one of the monkey fists, she frowned. "Maybe I shouldn't have chosen this rope knot."

He knew what she was talking about, but he shook his

head. "No worries, Bree. Those knots were used a very long time ago. They don't hold any memories for me, good or bad."

Her shoulders visibly relaxed. "Good."

"Want something to drink? I have soda. Water."

"A water would be great, thanks."

He grabbed her a bottle from the fridge as she sat on one of the tall stools. Handing it to her, he leaned on the low counter at his back. "I'm cooking tonight."

Her eyes went round. "Get out."

"I am, but I'm not making any promises."

"Hmm, let me guess. Steak? Or steak?"

"I'm an evolved male. I bought salmon."

"Did you buy veggies?"

"I did."

She hopped off the stool. "Then I'll make the salad."

As they worked together it felt very normal. Domestic, even. He wouldn't worry about it. Yes, they were working in easy compatibility in his kitchen but pretty soon they would take that up to his new bed in the master bedroom.

They ate their dinner and afterwards sat on his sectional. "This is a really nice piece. You needed something big to fill this space."

"Size again?"

She laughed, her brows raised. "It surprises me every time you make a joke, Derek."

"Because I have a stick up my ass?"

"Now, before you get offended that was just your reputation."

"So I had a reputation of being a dick?"

"Not a dick, precisely." She came closer and kissed his cheek. "No one really knew you, that's all."

Her words had him thinking. That was deliberate. Keeping to himself. From years of putting up a front.

"Now that you know me?" He tucked a strand of hair behind her ear. "What do you think?"

She came up on her knees and placed her hands on his cheeks. "You're Derek. Just Derek." Her cheeks were pink again. "I can't explain it."

He kissed her, softly so that their lips clung for a second as he pulled away. "You don't have to."

She took one of his hands in hers, tugging as she came to her feet. "Show me the rest of your new house, Derek."

He felt that rush again. The want and hunger for only this woman. They were both avoiding putting any sort of label on what this was. Hell, they weren't even talking about that avoidance. But right now?

Right now he couldn't even think about how many fucks he didn't give.

***

Bree's eyes popped open and she stared at the tray ceiling in Derek's bedroom. They'd spent the entire day together yesterday, again, and today was her father's party. The screen on her phone showed it was just past five o'clock, but her mind was going in circles.

Covering her face with her hands, she took in a long deep breath. She knew just who would be there. Her father's associates and their families. Couples from the country club and their adult children. Ugh, Kip would most definitely be there.

He'd dated her for the sole reason of getting close to her father, after all. What a dick. And she'd thought Derek had been that way? Kip was a completely different kind of asshole without equal.

"Why are you awake, baby?" Derek asked in a sleep-roughened voice.

She turned her head to find him gazing at her. His eyes were a little unfocused, his cheeks showing dark stubble, but he looked hot. Any thoughts of Kip and his grasping ways flew out of her head.

"Just thinking about today," was all she would say about the guest list.

He rubbed a hand over his face. "Are you that worried?"

She blew out a breath. "Not really worried. I just want to be prepared, you know?"

"No. I don't." He turned, resting his head on one hand. "Tell me."

The setting was very intimate, like it had been in the tub at the inn. In the semi-dark, she could confess what had happened at her father's last party.

"It was a year ago," she said. "May Day."

"The same day," Derek said. "At you father's party?"

"Yes." She turned, folding her hands under one cheek as she faced him. "I was seeing this guy, Kip. Sort of. Anyway, my mother and father wanted us to be together. My grandmother had died just two months before and I'd taken the job at Cypress. They told me I was drifting."

"Drifting." His lips thinned. "Go on."

"Kip got me alone in my father's study." She held up a hand. "Before you even think it, nothing happened. He didn't try to force anything or profess his undying love for me."

"So he's a dick but not an asshole."

That made her laugh a little. "Pretty much. He had this idea, though. Why not get married and make our parents happy?"

"What? That's archaic."

"At the very least. He was seeing someone at the time, too. Someone I don't think his parents liked very much."

"This is all so...icky."

"Icky? Never thought I'd hear you say that, but yeah it was."

"What did you do?"

"Told him to go to Hell."

"That's my girl."

She let that little nickname slide without comment. "He told my father that he proposed and I turned him down."

"Is that the reason your parents are mad at you?"

She nodded. "That and the fact that I took my grandmother's inheritance and got the heck out of Dodge. Or Heathrow. The Kip thing was the icing on the cake."

"You haven't tried to explain it? Never mind. You're their daughter. They should have known what was going on."

"They thought Kip and I were dating. I was hardly speaking to them at the time, so I never bothered to straighten out the mess. Then it only got messier."

"This Kip guy." Derek rolled onto his back and folded his hands beneath his head. "He's going to be there today, isn't he?"

"I'm sure he will be."

"And how do you feel about that?"

She tried to figure out just what he was asking her. "I never even liked him, Derek."

He turned his head and smiled. "Good. Then we have nothing to worry about."

Her mouth dropped open. "How can you say that?"

"Baby, I've been to hundreds of these events. All of my life. I know how to act but I can be a son-of-a-bitch if I have to be. Sounds like this Kip guy might need a talking-to."

She groaned. "Please, don't. I love that you'd do that for me, though."

It hung there. The L-word. He closed his eyes and nodded. "Then get a couple more hours of sleep. We'll deal with this later."

Relieved, she settled against his side and let his even breathing and the steady rise and fall of his chest rock her to sleep.

A while later, she stood in front of her closet. After waking her up at a more decent hour in a very naughty and memorable way, Derek fed her breakfast and sent her on home to dress. The party would start at noon, and there was no way she could be late.

Her encounter with Kip last year, and her disclosure of it to Derek, should have embarrassed her but she was already feeling stronger. Just knowing Derek would have her back, whatever that might entail, was enough to give her the courage to get through this darn day.

After showering in her own place, she chose a sheath dress of light beige. It had a lace overlay of sky blue and the hem came to just above her knees. It was May first, not Memorial Day after all, so she slipped on a pair of strappy beige high-heeled sandals. After blow-drying her hair, she'd left it long and straight, so it fell to her shoulder blades. Her mother's blond hair would be wound tight in an up-do, which was another reason to leave hers down.

She hardly wore makeup at work, but she put in a little more effort today. Everyone would be studying her, of course. She was Arthur and Margaret's only child. A touch of mascara, a sweep of blush, a dollop of lip gloss and she was ready.

A few minutes later Derek rang the doorbell and was waiting on her porch. Whoa, he looked good. He wore an expensive yet understated suit and his hair was as neat as she'd ever seen it. In the recent past she might have thought he looked like the uptight jerk she used to think he was. Today? Today he was smoking hot and stole her breath.

"You clean up really nice, Derek."

He smiled and his hotness factor rose exponentially. "And you look… Damn, are you naked under that lace?"

"It's an illusion." She twirled a little. "See?"

"I see a zipper I'm going to pull down later."

She laughed and stepped aside to let him in. "I know what you're doing."

"And what's that?"

"Taking my mind off the coming crap storm."

"Just breathe, baby. Your parents want to see you. That's all."

She shook her head. "You don't know them like I do."

"Maybe not, but I know the type. Just nod and smile and then we can get the hell out of there."

"Don't tempt me. We have to stay through the meal but we

can leave before the dancing starts."

"There's going to be dancing?"

He looked horrified but she knew that was a front, too. "You can dance, can't you?"

"Yes. Sorry."

"Well, you won't have to today."

"If you say so. Are you just about ready?"

She nodded and picked up her small tan leather clutch. Locking the front door behind her, she headed down the front walk to Derek's waiting Lexus.

He opened her door and stood there, his head tilted to one side. "What?"

"I was just thinking that I couldn't have ordered a better date for this thing."

He smiled. "Don't even think about ordering any kind of date. You're stuck with me."

His words tumbled through her mind. What did he mean by that?

Taking his words at face value, she shrugged. "Good to know."

They left Cypress, headed for the interstate and the long drive to Heathrow.

Chapter 15

Bree was fidgeting, her knees going up and down as he drove toward Orlando. She looked gorgeous in that blue dress that made her look like she was naked underneath, but her posture was rigid and her jaw clenched.

"Breathe, baby." He settled a hand on her left thigh, almost ignoring how silky-smooth her skin was beneath his fingertips. "It's just a party. Keep telling yourself that."

She looked at him, blowing out a breath as she nodded. "It's just a party. Okay. I can do this."

"I'm going to be there, too."

She shook her head. "I'm sorry I asked you to come. Oh, not that I don't want you there. I do!"

"Bree, try to chill. Even just a little. We'll see your parents. Eat some hors d'oeuvres. Drink some wine. Easy-peasy."

She gave a delicate little snort. "If you say so."

He gave her leg a pat and took his hand from her. "Trust me. No matter how hard it gets, we can leave. Just go."

Her leg started to jiggle again and she spread her own hand on her knee. "Promise?"

"On my honor."

"Okay." She blew out another breath. "Good."

She directed him to take the next exit and he followed the rest of her instructions through what was clearly a very exclusive part of Orlando. They drove past houses that he couldn't see from the road. Most were walled in and protected by iron gates. The lush grass and meticulously-landscaped shrubs would look right at home in Brookline, Massachusetts. Eddie had wanted to keep the house in the divorce, but Derek knew what that house was worth and there had been no way in Hell he would let Eddie keep it.

Their mother had made the house a home when he and Abby had been growing up, no small feat considering how big and ostentatious it was. Once he, and then Abby, had moved out it became his mother's prison. She had been little more than an employee, hosting his father's dinners and directing his staff. Now that she was living in the home without Eddie, he hoped she was learning to just be herself. For herself. And when he moved her to Cypress he would make certain she kept the house if she still wanted it.

"Here." Bree pointed to the left. "That's the drive."

He'd been so wrapped up in his mother's situation he'd almost forgotten where they were headed today. He pulled into the drive and past the iron gates. These were thrown wide open, no doubt welcoming the guests for today's event.

"Oh, boy," Bree whispered.

Once past the gates, the property opened up in a big way. The grounds were more extensive than his family home's, which could be expected since here they had the luxury of land that wasn't always the case up north. The long drive was set with paver stones and led to a courtyard with a fountain in the center. Derek pulled up near the home, taking in the three story estate home. It was done in Spanish Mediterranean, with squat columns and miles of curved tiles on the peaks of the roof.

"Nice digs," he teased.

She slid him a smile. "Right?"

A valet opened Bree's door and she stepped out onto the drive. Derek handed the guy his key when he hurried around to his side and stepped over to stand very close to Bree.

There were lots of cars on the drive and as they turned to face the wide entry she froze.

"Ready, baby?" he whispered.

She straightened her shoulders and gave a nod. He'd seen this particular move of hers before. He was beginning to think of it as her power stance.

Placing his hand on the small of her back, he gave her a

gentle push. "Then let's do this."

The place was a crush, with very nicely dressed people milling about and talking. They ranged in age from twenties up to sixties, if he had to guess. There was the impression of space from the soaring ceiling above the tiled entry, and the house was well decorated. A sweeping staircase curved upward from the entry to a gallery above. Servers circulated with trays of tiny fried, baked or stacked things and others carried flutes of champagne.

"Do you want me to grab you a drink?" he asked.

She shook her head. "Not yet."

Not yet. That sounded ominous. "Your call."

"Sabrina," a woman called from the staircase.

Derek saw a woman who looked a lot like Bree glide toward them. Her eyes were the same stunning blue as Bree's, but hers appeared guarded and a little cold.

"Hi, Mom."

Bree's voice was laced with something Derek might call fear if he didn't know her so well by now. She was apprehensive, but she didn't fear her mother.

The woman grasped Bree by her shoulders and air-kissed her cheek. Stepping back, she regarded Derek. "And whom do we have here?"

"Derek Stone, ma'am." Derek held out his hand which she took with her own. Her touch was as chilly as her eyes. "I'm a friend of your daughter's."

"Margaret James." She dropped his hand. "How long have you been a friend of my daughter's?"

"Mom," Bree put in.

"I'm just asking." Her gaze slid away from Derek and as he watched he saw the wary affection the woman had for Bree. "How is Cypress Corners?"

"It's good, thanks."

"And your job? Is it going well?"

Bree nodded. "Very well, thank you."

"Bree handled my recent house purchase," Derek put in.

Mrs. James arched a brow at him. "Oh? You live in Cypress as well?"

He nodded. "I do."

"And what do you do there?"

"Mom," Bree said again.

"Sabrina, I'm curious."

Bree and her mother stared at each other for a long minute. Derek fought the urge to ring a bell so they could come out fighting. Both women were slight. Delicate looking, but fierce. The guests milling about appeared mildly curious, but from having attended these kinds of events in the past Derek guessed they were more concerned with their own jockeying for positions in this social setting. No one was going to come between a mother and her daughter. Not in their family home.

"Sabrina, you came." A tall, broad man with salt-and-pepper hair strode toward them. "Welcome home."

***

Bree turned to her father, biting back the retort that she wasn't home. This was strictly a visit, a required one and one that wouldn't be repeated until Thanksgiving at the earliest.

"Hello, Dad."

To her shock he enveloped her in a hug. She kept her hands at her sides, at a loss. This was new. When he released her she blinked up at him. The smile he wore put her on her guard.

"It's so good to see you." He turned to Derek. "And whom do we have here?" he asked, echoing her mother's very question.

Bree shot Derek a look of apology before she made the introductions this time. "Dad, this is Derek Stone. Derek, this is my father. Arthur James."

The two men shook hands, holding on for a long minute as

her father clearly sized up Derek. Poor Derek. He hadn't signed on for this baloney.

"It's very nice to meet you, Mr. James." Derek was the first to break their hold, clearly in deference to her father. "You have a lovely home."

"Thank you." Her father's blue eyes narrowed. "Stone. Hmm. Do I hear a Boston accent?"

"A bit, I'm afraid."

"You live in Cypress."

Bree started to tell him to leave Derek alone but Derek held up a hand.

"I do, sir. I work there as well."

"You do." It wasn't a question but Derek apparently knew the unspoken rule of fatherly interference.

"I'm the in-house counsel for the development."

Her father looked impressed. "In-house counsel. Stone. From Boston."

"Are you compiling a dossier, Dad?" Bree asked.

To her astonishment, her father laughed. "Maybe. Derek, are you related to the Stone law firm in Boston?"

Derek's lips thinned but he nodded. "I am."

"A very respectable firm."

"Yes."

Her father beamed another smile in Bree's direction.

"Please mingle, Sabrina. Take Derek and enjoy yourselves."

Bree's mouth dropped open. "Thanks, Dad. We will."

Her mother gave her a searching look, but it didn't feel nearly as judgmental as her usual scrutiny. Together the older couple headed further into the crowded party to meet and greet their guests.

"That was strange," she whispered.

Derek shrugged. "What, the inquisition?"

Bree couldn't put what she was feeling into words. Her father didn't do hugs. He certainly didn't do warmth. She just gave a small shake of her head.

"Don't worry about it." The smile Derek gave her was small but bolstered her. "It's a father thing."

Oh. The inquisition. That was something from her father that wasn't out of character.

"You've been on the receiving end of that kind of thing before?"

"Not me. But if I had a daughter you better believe I'd question the hell out of any guy who wanted to date her."

She caught what he meant even if he didn't say it out loud.

His father was abusive. Derek was protective of his mother and sister. He would be on the lookout for any signs of danger if he had a daughter.

Her belly clenched. He would make a wonderful father with that wide streak of protectiveness.

"Now, your mother is another story."

Bree laughed, as he'd obviously expected her to. "She seemed to like you."

"What's not to like?"

She placed her hand on his sleeve and tilted her head toward the main salon. "Let's get this over with."

"Lead on, Sabrina."

Shooting him a glare, she saw the smile teasing his lips. "Watch it, Due Diligence."

"There she is," she said, lifting her chin toward a large portrait hanging over the mantle in the parlor. "My grandmother."

Derek stared up at the painting, his eyes wide. "You look a lot like her."

"I know."

"She was beautiful."

"Thank you for that."

213

"It's true. There's more to it, though. She looks like she has strength." He took her hand in his. "Like you."

She just smiled. *If only.*

As they entered the main party area she recognized a few of her father's associates and her mother's friends. Kip's parents were here, of course. They never missed a chance to sit at her father's table.

"There's Bitsy and Chip," she said in a low voice.

Derek arched a brow. "You're not serious."

That made her smile. "Don't even tell me that you didn't grow up around a Muffy, a Chip, a Skip… I can go on."

"Please, don't. Yes, the white elite tends to pick the most ridiculous of nicknames." Derek finally snagged them a couple of drinks. "Here. To Buffy and Skip."

She sipped, letting the bubbly wine tickle her nose. The sting and strangeness of her mother's probing stares and her father's interrogation began to recede. "Like water off a duck's back."

"Hey, there." He nudged her with his shoulder. "Nautical references are my thing."

"Ducks are nautical?"

"They swim, don't they?"

She started to say something when she spied Kip walking towards them. "Oh, God."

Derek's dark eyes narrowed as her sort-of ex came closer.

"Bree, you look hot," Kip said.

She rolled her eyes. "Ever the charmer."

Kip winked and turned to Derek. She compared the two men in a quick minute. Kip came out on the losing end of that match-up. Long-limbed and slender, Kip had the blond Arian preppy thing going for him, from his Hilfiger polo to his Topsiders. He was clean-shaven and his hair was swept back from his forehead.

"Kip, this is Derek," she said.

"Derek…" Kip began.

"Stone." Derek kept his hands at his sides. "Chip, is it?"

Kip's fair cheeks turned pink. "Kip."

"That's better, I guess."

Bree swallowed a laugh. The social niceties were so ingrained in her she had to ask after him. "How are you, Kip?"

"Stellar, darling." Kip flashed that phony smile of his, his teeth big and white. "Seems that your jilting me made me a bit of an oddity." He shot Derek a sharp look. "Seems no one could imagine why any girl would refuse me."

"All right," Derek put in.

Kip bristled and faced Bree again. "It seems that the girls in our crowd wanted to take care of me. Soothe my hurt feelings, and what not."

She cringed. "Spare me, please."

Kip's patrician nose when straight in the air. "Nevertheless, I'm in high demand now. So I thank you, Bree."

"I'm so glad I could help." Her tone was chilly now, but Kip was so self-absorbed he didn't catch on. "If you'll excuse us?"

Derek apparently didn't have to be told twice. He took Bree's elbow and steered her away from the braying ass. Kip gaped at them but when Derek began to rub his thumb on the inside of her elbow she soothed a little. Caught a little heat, too. Breathing in Derek's scent, she rid herself of Kip as easily as that proverbial duck shed water.

"That guy is a dick," Derek said.

"I know. When you called yourself one a few weeks ago, you were definitely misguided."

He smiled, bright and hot at the same time. "Thank you."

She covered his hand with hers, stroking the backs of his long fingers. "And thank you for that."

He stared into her eyes and she felt like tumbling into their depths. Of running from her parents' party and falling into his new big bed in his new big house.

"Keep looking at me like that and I might have to compromise your virtue in the study."

She laughed out loud. "Why, Derek Stone! How outrageous."

His smile turned warm and easy and she felt lighter.

"Come on, Bree." He reached up to brush her hair over her shoulder, letting his fingers stroke over her collar bone. "Let's get something to eat. Miles to go before we can escape."

"No joke." She sighed as Kip's parents wound their way through the crowd toward them. "Let's get this over with."

"I'm right here."

Her heart tripped at his words. "Thank you again."

She shouldn't need a man at her side. She didn't, which was one reason she'd refused to have anything with Kip's arrangement last year. This man, though?

With Derek she could imagine staying at his side forever. It wasn't what they were, though. It wasn't what they would become. Her heart might have a different idea but her head knew what was what.

Still, for the next couple of hours she would lean on him as much as she liked. Looking up at the portrait of her grandmother, she winked. *Take your power where you can.* It was one of her grandmother's favorite sayings, and Bree would follow that advice today.

Her heart and head could argue about this tomorrow.

Chapter 16

"So this is Cypress Corners."

Derek smiled at his mother. "It is."

When she'd called him Monday morning with her itinerary, he'd been surprised. Still, he'd taken Wednesday afternoon off to pick her up from Orlando International Airport. After the strangeness that had been Bree's parents' party, it was only fitting that he would bring his own family drama to Cypress Corners.

From the second he'd picked his mother up she'd been talking nonstop. She seemed more like Abby than his mother right now, and it was a very welcome change.

He turned the Lexus into the entrance, down the long drive bracketed by white ranch fencing and tall leafy trees that led them towards the center of town.

"This doesn't look anything like I imagined."

"And just what did you imagine?"

"Oh, I don't know. Something like the Florida Keys. Or maybe Miami. Not this small town look. It reminds me of the little places we would visit up in New England. Even the trees, Derek. I don't see any palm trees."

"I think they call this Old Florida, Mom."

"How old is this place?"

"Not even twenty years old, believe it or not. They're going to build a gazebo in the center over there." He pointed toward the right of the Cypress Institute. "I'm sure it won't look brand new, either."

"You like it here, don't you?"

Derek glanced over at her. "I do."

"Abby said you seemed different."

"Yes, I know. She called me Cypress Derek."

His mother laughed. "I wanted her to come with me but she's intent on working out her notice."

"A month, though?" Derek scoffed. "Her boss doesn't deserve that."

"Still, she's a lot like you. Dedicated."

He made some sort of noncommittal sound. Dedication was pretty much all he'd had when he'd broken away from his father. When he'd decided not to even clerk in Eddie's firm. If someone gave him a chance, he paid them back tenfold. His relationship with Bill Chapman was like that. One of mutual respect and a whole lot of dedication on Derek's side of the equation.

"Now, what is this about the girl you're seeing?"

He kept his expression even. "Who?"

She clicked her tongue. "Abby told me you were seeing someone."

Derek searched his brain for any recollection of talking about Bree to Abby. Maybe he'd mentioned a dinner date or something.

"I am, but it's not serious."

"Yet."

"Yet?"

"You're a serious man, Derek. Sometimes I think you're too serious."

Did Bree think that, too? Yes, he'd had her back at the party on Sunday but after he'd had her back at his house he'd put all of that out of his mind. Had she?

"I want to meet her."

He blew out a breath. "All right. But please don't push."

"I don't push."

"If you say so."

She waved a hand. "I push Abby, Derek. Never you. I've never had to."

He took what she said as a compliment, even if she meant it as a reprimand. He'd had to be a self-starter. He wouldn't have gotten any encouragement from Eddie if he'd asked for it.

They were quiet at last as he drove towards his new house. He took in her appearance again. Her clothes were lighter, somehow. Not just in color. She wore a pair of tan cropped pants and a buttoned shirt in light orange. Her hair, dark and thick like all of them had, was shiny and cut to brush her jawline. Her eyes were bright, too. Sharp, so he should be careful when he introduced her to Bree. It wouldn't do for either woman to get any ideas of just where this relationship thing was going.

"Is that your house?" his mother asked. "It needs to be painted."

He chuckled. "Yes and yes."

He steered around to the driveway set at the back of the house and pulled into the garage. Turning off the engine, he faced her. "I'm glad you're here, Mom."

She hugged him fiercely. "I'm so glad you're finding a place, Derek."

He pulled back, searching her face. "For you?"

She shook her head. "No. For you."

His throat tightened but he pushed past any emotions by getting out and grabbing her suitcases from the trunk.

"We can go out to dinner tonight, if you like. I think you'll like the Clubhouse."

She wrinkled her nose. "That big place I saw at the top of the town square? No. What about a little place, Derek? That bakery, maybe? The coffee shop?"

He opened the door for her and followed her through the mudroom and into the kitchen. "The bakery is closed by now and the coffee shop doesn't really have anything for dinner." He set her suitcases down. "How about the Town Tavern?"

"That sounds fun! Darts and beer?"

He stared at her. "Who are you?"

She shrugged. "It's a tavern. It sounds like it would have darts and beer."

"I guess it does."

"You haven't eaten there?"

"I have. Often, actually."

"With your not-serious someone?"

"Mom, please."

She walked through the house, looking at his new furniture and the way the place was arranged. "Your house is lovely. Who helped you with the decorating?"

"How do you know I had help?"

She arched a brow, an expression he knew he'd gotten

from her. "I've seen your apartments in Boston, remember. All of them. Very little warmth there."

"I had help," was all he'd say.

She started up the stairs. "Just show me my room, son."

"I thought you might want to be down here."

"I'm not feeble, Derek."

"I know." From just the little time they'd spent together this afternoon he suspected she was a lot stronger than he'd thought. "But there's a guest suite."

"Oh, okay. When your sister gets down here, she can take that."

"There are guest rooms upstairs, too."

"You bought a family home."

He shrugged. "It made good financial sense."

She snorted again. "All right, then. I'll leave it alone." She grabbed one of her suitcases and pulled up the long handle. "Make reservations at this tavern of yours, Derek." She rolled her bag down the hallway behind her. "And call your not-serious friend. I want to meet her."

Derek knew it was silly to argue with his mother on this. He put the rest of her bags in her guest suite and returned to the great room. He could hear her humming, and was very happy she liked the room. Drawing out his phone he texted Bree.

Dinner tonight? Heads up, my mother's here.

Yeah? Okay, I owe you.

Grinning, he answered her.

7 at the tavern. Come prepared.

You can't scare me. Not after Sunday. C U later.

He set his phone on the counter and opened the fridge.

"Tell me you're not serious," his mother said.

He swung the refrigerator door closed and found his mother standing there. "What?"

"I saw your face, Derek."

His lips thinned. "She'll join us for dinner, Mom. That's all I'll say."

She beamed, clasping her hands. "That's all I need to hear."

***

Bree walked into the tavern, facing Joy at the hostess stand. "Yes, I'm meeting someone."

Joy grinned. "Let me guess."

Bree shook her head. "Derek is meeting me here with his mother."

Joy gaped at her. "Seriously?"

225

"Why would anyone make that up?"

"I thought you might be playing with me."

"Are they here?"

"No, but he made a reservation for three."

"Then why are you playing with me?"

"Payback."

Bree rolled her eyes. "I'll be at the bar."

Joy nodded. "You'll need it."

"You know, not everyone's mother is like yours."

"Thank God for that. Speaking of which, how did your big family party go on Sunday?"

"You knew about that?"

"Oliver was in here for lunch."

"That guy likes his gossip."

"So it went all right?"

"It did, actually." No small thanks went to Derek for that. "And now I don't have to go back there until Thanksgiving."

"I wish I could say that. It looks like I'll be stuck at the inn for the foreseeable future."

"Sorry, girl. But hey, you have unlimited access to those cinnamon rolls."

"Somehow I think that cinnamon rolls in the lobby aren't

quite the same as cinnamon rolls on a room service cart." Joy winked. "Am I right?"

Bree flushed but managed to shrug. "I'll be at the bar," she said again.

"Can I get a glass of water?" she asked the bartender. The guy nodded and she sat on a stool.

As she sipped, she tried to put Joy's words out of her mind. Still, that first weekend she'd spent with Derek in his room at the inn would be very hard to forget. Hot, sexy Derek was a lot to take after all. The sweet, strong Derek she'd been with before, during and after her parents' party was even more compelling. Now she was meeting his mother?

Turning away from the bar, she watched for Derek and his mother. She easily spotted the woman when she walked up to Joy. She had Derek's dark hair and she was taller than Bree's mother. Joy pointed in Bree's direction and then she spied eyes just like Derek's in a pretty, heart-shaped face.

"Hello, dear. You must be Derek's friend."

Bree smiled at her. "Bree James, ma'am."

"Ma'am? Please call me Susan."

"Susan." She shook his mother's hand. "It's very nice to meet you."

227

"And you. I hear you helped Derek with his house?"

"I handled the sale, yes."

"Oh? That I didn't know. I meant with the decorating."

Bree nearly bit her tongue. "I did."

Derek joined them, placing a hand on his mother's shoulder. "Don't give Bree the third degree."

"Don't give me your lawyer speak, son."

Bree laughed and his mother grinned. "He can be a little, oh what's the word? Serious?"

Derek seemed to pick up something from his mother's statement, but it was lost on her.

"He can be," Bree said.

Derek's mother slanted him a look and Bree decided she liked this woman. She was spunky.

Joy came over to them. "Your table is ready."

They followed her, settling at a table near the fireplace.

"I don't see a dartboard," Susan said.

"A dartboard?"

"It looks like a pub, Bree. Shouldn't there be a dartboard?"

"It sounds like Derek needs to take you to the End Zone in St. Cloud. They have pool and games and several dartboards."

"Sounds like my kind of place," his mother said with a

smile.

"Since when?" Derek asked, an expression of dismay on his face.

"You've been gone for almost two months, son. I've changed."

A smile tugged at his mouth. "I see that. It looks good."

Bree caught the undercurrent of affection and the unasked question about his father. If his mother was moving past what had to be a horrific marriage, Bree could only give her props.

Their meal was peppered with light conversation, but all through dinner Derek's mother was clearly sizing her up. Bree didn't begrudge her. Hadn't Derek dealt with that and more at her parents' party?

Afterwards, they stood out on the concrete steps in front of the tavern. They made their way towards a sculpted metal bench shaped to resemble a dragonfly.

"This is pretty," his mother said. "I noticed there are a lot of artistic pieces around the square."

"There are," Bree said. "Local artists just love this place."

"And you do, too," Susan said.

"I do."

"How long have you lived here?"

"It was a year this past April."

Susan nodded. "There's something here. I can feel it."

Derek looked stunned but he covered it with that mask she hadn't noticed in a couple of weeks. "What's that?"

"In Cypress, dear." She raised her brows in Bree's direction. "I wonder what he thought I meant?"

Bree stifled a laugh. "There's no telling, Susan."

Derek growled a little at her but smiled. "And on that note, why don't I get you home Mom?"

"You can drive me home, but you'd better go to Bree's afterwards."

Bree's jaw dropped. "What?"

"To say a proper good night, dear," his mother said. "It would be preferable if he were to drive you home but I don't dare drive that fancy car of his back to his house."

"Good night, Bree," Derek said.

Would he show up later? Under his mother's watchful eye, she doubted he would want to give the woman any encouragement in her meddling. She wanted to see Derek, though. They'd hardly spent a night apart since before this past weekend.

"Good night."

She made her way across the street to her Mustang. As always, sitting in the car made her feel like her grandmother was giving her a hug. Seeing her portrait again, after such a long time, gave Bree the courage to continue on her path. Speaking of her career and living arrangements, at least. Whatever she had going on with Derek was a completely different matter.

Her house felt empty when she walked in, but she crossed to the hope chest. There was little inside of it, except for some pretty linens and a few faded newspapers. Bree's father had the bulk of the woman's belongings of the legal variety at least. Bree inherited money and the storage unit contents, and that suited her just fine.

She kicked off her shoes as she made her way upstairs to her bedroom. Dinner with Derek and his mother had been very nice, but she couldn't help but wish he had his house to himself tonight. She had her house, of course.

Changing into her pajama pants and a long-sleeved T, she resigned herself to a lonely night. It wasn't like she and Derek had any sort of understanding. They'd spent nearly every night together over the past few weeks. That was true. Still, they each had their own lives, didn't they?

Back downstairs, she flicked on the TV. One of those

shows where the guy gives a different girl a rose every night was on, so she idly watched and zoned out. When her doorbell rang, she jumped. Her heartbeat followed suit, and she knew who would be standing on her porch.

Her pulse tripping, she opened the door and found Derek there. His eyes were dark and questioning.

"Bree?"

She knew what he was asking. Smiling wide, she nodded.

Chapter 17

Derek felt the impact of Bree's silent agreement, and it was like lightning struck. Stepping into her house, he wrapped his arms around her. He hadn't realized how much he'd needed to hold her, to kiss her, until he'd seen her open her door. Cupping her face, he brought his mouth to hers and tasted her. She was soft and pliant in his hold, and he let his hands roam all over her. Her perfect ass. Her soft skin. Her silky hair.

She kissed him back, wrapping herself around him as he slid his hands up the back of her shirt. Her breath hitched and she shivered against him.

"Upstairs," she breathed.

She didn't have to ask him twice. He got her in her bed, naked, and stretched out for him almost before he could count to ten. He tasted her all over now, using his lips and his tongue to drive her crazy. She purred, a hungry needy sound, and he was so hard he was ready to burst.

"I have to get inside you, baby." He kissed her beautiful mouth again, letting her feel just how far gone he was. Her skin was hot against him. Wet. "Now."

"Please," she urged.

He grabbed a condom from her nightstand, he'd put the

box there himself last week, and took care of it.

He rubbed his mouth against her throat, nipping gently. "This is going to be fast, Bree."

"Fast or slow," she panted. "Don't care."

He shifted and entered her, taking a heart-stopping second to revel in how right she fit him. How perfect. Her hands were tight on his arms as he started to move, her body bowed back as she took all of him. He wasn't inexperienced. Not by a long shot. But he'd had Bree so many different ways over the past few weeks, he couldn't remember what any other woman's body felt like. Tasted like.

She was sobbing now, saying his name as she neared her release. His head was filled with her and, closing his eyes, he drove himself over the edge and took her with him.

After, he fell to his side next to her. "God, Bree."

She sighed, turning to tuck herself up against his side the way he was really starting to like. "Nice to see you, Derek."

He laughed low in his throat. "I didn't mean to rush you, baby."

"Mmm, I'm not complaining." She nuzzled his neck, another thing he really liked. "I thought this wouldn't happen tonight."

"Me, too." He ran his fingers through her hair, straightening the mess he'd made of it. "My mother practically threw me out of the house."

She smiled up at him, her eyes sparkling. "I like your mother."

He shifted a little, drawing her closer. "So we've met each other's mothers."

"Yeah."

"What does that mean, exactly?"

She turned, stacking her hands beneath her chin as she furrowed her brow. "I've met plenty of guys' parents, Derek. This doesn't have to mean a thing."

He wondered about that for a minute, thinking about that dick Kip and his ice-cold parents, and then shook his head. "I've never met a girl's parents."

"Truly? I mean, I know you said that you hadn't been interrogated by a father before. But, never?"

"My relationships were never about more than what they were."

"What does that mean?"

What did that mean? "Casual, I guess. Only once in a while. I don't know. I didn't really date."

"You?" She stroked the center of his chest, her fingers working in a small circle. "But, how is that possible? You're gorgeous."

"Thank you for that, but I think that's the orgasm talking."

She laughed softly, dipping her head to kiss his bicep. "I feel too good right now to argue with you."

"That's a shame. You know how much I like to argue."

She nodded. "Due Diligence."

They laid there, just breathing and gently stroking each other until he found himself needing her again. This time she took the lead, climbing on top and riding him until he thought he'd pass out from his climax. Holding her tight against his chest, he let himself breathe her deep inside.

"What is this, Bree?"

"What?"

"Us."

She jerked her head up so fast she knocked him in the chin. "Us?"

He'd bitten his tongue, so he took a few seconds to answer. "Yes, us. What are we doing?"

She pushed herself up on her arms, and he took a long look at her plump and rosy breasts before meeting her gaze.

"We're dating, Derek. That's what we're doing."

"All right."

"Where is this coming from?" She slid off of him, gathering the sheets over her as she folded her knees beneath her. "We never talked about this before."

"I know." He brushed his hair back from his face, blowing out a breath. "This is all new to me. I'm sorry."

"Hey, no sorries remember?"

He found a smile. "God, that conversation feels like eons ago."

"Just a few weeks, actually."

"I don't want to fuck this up, Bree. Whatever this is."

"Then we'll just go on as we have been. No expectations. I've had them in the past and no one ever ended up happy."

He'd never had any expectations. Not as far as relationships were concerned anyway. There were a few things he wondered about, though.

"Are you seeing anyone else?" he had to know.

She blinked at him and then flashed a cute smile. "I'm not. The guy I'm seeing keeps me way too happy."

He let out a breath he hadn't been aware he was holding. "Then this is exclusive."

"Unless you're seeing Lettie, I'd say so."

Grinning, he shook his head.

"You really are clueless about this," she added.

"I am." He grabbed her and turned to pin her beneath him. "But I'm a very fast learner."

The mood was considerably lighter as they focused on making each other feel rather than think. It was only later, when Derek was back home stretched out alone in his big bed, that he realized he'd asked for a sort-of commitment from Bree. And gotten it, amazingly. She wasn't seeing any other guy and he'd told her he only wanted to see her. Not in so many words, which was a first for him about…anything.

No expectations. No obligations. Then why did he feel like he was missing something?

***

"So what's up with you and Mr. Tall, dark and not-so-gloomy?" Oliver asked when she arrived back at her desk the next afternoon.

"I guess we're dating, Ollie."

"You guess?" He smirked at her. "Then you're doing it wrong."

Bree waved a hand. "It's early days."

"It took the Pixie all of a week to fall for Noah."

"Jessie was half in love with Noah from the day he came to Cypress."

"Mmm, weren't we all?"

"Um, no. Still, Derek and I are not Noah and Jessie."

"And none of you are me and Todd." Ollie shrugged. "So what?"

"I've been out at the model home all morning, Ollie." Bree tried to make sense of Oliver's circular logic. "What are you asking me?"

"I met Derek Stone's mother this morning, she is such a lovely lady, and she mentioned having dinner with you and Derek last night."

"We did."

"She also mentioned her son staying out afterwards."

Bree swallowed, fixing a cool expression on her heated face. "Is Lettie saving you a seat at her table this afternoon?"

Oliver laughed. "I'm just happy you're getting some. I was worried."

"I don't need you to be my hookup fairy godfather," she said. "Aren't you supposed to be in charge of Tammy's life?"

He snorted. "She's so happy with her very own Chapman

there's absolutely no drama there."

"I'm sorry for your loss."

Oliver gaped at her, and then grinned. "Bree James, throwing shade?"

"No. Just asking for you to leave the subject of my love life out of your field of expertise."

"You've got it, girl." He held up splayed hands. "Just making conversation."

"Oh, I can't be mad at you Ollie. You're a sweetie."

"I am."

With that, Oliver hurried over to his desk and settled down in front of his laptop. Shaking her head, Bree hid behind her own computer and clicked through the afternoon's coming appointments.

As she reviewed her schedule, she couldn't help but think about Derek. Not that what Oliver said bothered her. She and Derek knew what was what and everyone else could jump in the lake. Still, he'd driven her crazy in more ways than one last night.

What the heck was up with that conversation? Derek, her perfect, in-the-moment kind of guy, wanted to be exclusive? She'd been stunned, and had she been completely in control of her faculties she would have questioned just what the heck had brought that on? His mother's arrival couldn't explain all of it.

She'd sensed something ever since he'd gone with her to her parents' party. Something very tempting. She'd leaned on him and it had felt so right she'd had little trouble imagining doing that forever. She so didn't do forever. She hadn't done it to make her parents happy and she wouldn't do it to make anyone else happy. Even if the guy was perfect for her in every way.

Her fingers froze on the keyboard. Since when did she think of him that way? Yes, he was perfect. Perfectly gorgeous and perfectly wonderful in bed. But perfect for her?

"No," she murmured. "That's crazy."

"What's crazy, Bree?" Oliver asked without looking up from his desk.

"N-nothing." She took a breath, her heart racing.

This felt a lot like when Kip had proposed his ridiculous idea last year. Like things were out of her control. Derek wasn't pushing her, though. And he certainly wasn't an idiot like Kip. Still, she felt like she was being forced. Forced to be something she wasn't. She so wasn't any guy's girlfriend. She never had been.

Derek had never dated before? She sure had. Tons of dates with tons of guys who never meant a thing. What she had with Derek, though? It was dating. Real, exclusive dating. That, truly, was a first for her.

Putting a hand over her chest, she breathed slowly in and out. Why hadn't she taken more yoga classes? Then she could refresh. Or revive. Or something like that.

"Mr. Forbes called a meeting," Jessie said as she rushed in. "Something about the launch."

Bree silently thanked Jessie for giving her something else to focus on at the moment. "What time?" she asked as she pulled up her schedule.

"Three thirty," Jessie said as her fingers flew over her keyboard. "That gives us just about twenty minutes."

Bree was only half listening now. She had her own stuff going on, but now she could turn her attention to something completely unrelated to her situation with Derek.

"Let's go, let's go!" Jessie grabbed a notebook and her tablet, bouncing on her feet. "Noah hasn't let me see any of Ben's plans, even though he's been working with him."

"Noah's been keeping secrets?"

"Only that one." Jessie tapped on Bree's desk. "Come on!"

Bree gathered her own things and closed her laptop. "Ollie, let's roll."

Oliver joined them and they made their way to the conference room. Bree stepped inside with a smile for Rick Chapman and Mr. Forbes. Then her gaze fell on Derek, standing just to the side of them. Her heart thudded and she knew. This was more than dating. This was even more than *exclusive* dating.

This was love, and she was in a lot of trouble.

Chapter 18

Derek took detailed notes on his tablet as Forbes and Rick related information regarding the launch. Eli presented more solidified plans as Ben and Noah each talked about what the Active Adult community would look like both in early days and upon completion of the first phase. It felt strange in a way, since last year he and Eli had been sent on an information-gathering mission. Now Derek was part of the team, as amazing as that should be. Aside from crew, he'd never been a part of any team. Not as a law clerk and not as a corporate lawyer.

Bree's gaze kept sliding to him, but he forced himself not to let her pretty blue eyes grab a hold of him. She looked worried about something, but that might just be her concentration face. There would be a lot of work involving the new village and, although she teased him about doing due diligence, she was very dedicated to her job.

After the meeting concluded, Derek reviewed his notes in the conference room. Absently saying good bye to the others, he sat at the long table for a few minutes.

"Everything all right, Derek?" Eli asked after everyone else had gone.

"Hmm? Yes, thanks. Just making sure my notes are

accurate."

"How about we get together tomorrow morning and review." Eli smiled. "I could use your, let's call it attention to detail."

Derek found a smile. "That would be great." He shut down his tablet and stood. "What are you up to tonight?"

"Early nights for Caro and me, man."

"You're totally committed, aren't you?"

"I am." Eli's brow furrowed. "What's going on with you and Bree?"

"Damned if I know." Derek blew out a breath. "This is all new for me."

"Dating in the fishbowl can suck, Derek. Trust me on this."

"Bree doesn't want people to know but I think that ship has left the dock."

Eli laughed. "Sail ho."

Derek shrugged. "I actually asked her where this was going."

Eli gaped at him. "Seriously?" He crossed to the door and closed it. "You started the conversation?"

"Shocked the hell out of myself, but yes."

"At the risk of sounding like Lettie, what was her answer?"

His belly tightened as he recalled the worry on her face. "Nothing. We're just going to go on as we are."

"Wow. That's good?"

"Are you asking me?"

"Most guys might want to just go with the flow, right?"

"Did you?"

Eli shook his head. "At first, maybe. Sure. What the hell did I know about relationships? Caro, though. She was even more afraid to get involved than I was."

"And now you're both fully committed and having a baby."

Eli flashed a wide smile. "Yep."

Derek doubted any such future was in the cards for him and Bree. She'd put him on notice last night and he wouldn't dare do anything to end what they had right now. Not before it ran its course, or whatever the hell happened.

He nodded at his friend but before Eli could tell him anything more about his reversal of fortune where emotional stuff was concerned he held up a hand. "Thanks, Eli."

Eli nodded. "I'll text you about tomorrow."

Derek nodded as Eli left the room. He'd never been at such a loss with a woman. Hell, he'd never really cared enough to bother to ask where they stood. He could see something more with Bree. Could feel something more.

He didn't give a shit about gossip or any of that. He did care about appearances, though. From years of hiding and crafting a finely-honed persona. Bree broke through it, amazingly. Pretty easily, too.

"Cypress Derek," he said to himself with a small smile. "Maybe there's something to that."

As he made his way back to his office his cell phone rang. Glancing at the screen, he saw that Bill Chapman was calling. He hadn't talked to him in a couple of weeks, so he was a little puzzled as he answered.

"Hello, Bill."

"Derek, I'm glad I caught you." Bill sounded abrupt, but he always was. "I assume you were in a meeting with Forbes?"

Derek didn't even ask how Bill knew that. "I was." He shut down his laptop and straightened his desk. "It just ended."

"I figured. The man loves his meetings." A soft chuckle came across the line, further baffling Derek. "This isn't about that, though."

"You don't want to know what was discussed about the new village?"

247

"I don't. Forbes will get with me on it, and you too. You'll see contracts coming soon, Derek. Chapman will be the main investor in the Active Adult community."

Derek grabbed his tablet and walked out of his office. "I bet you're happy."

"Ah, son. I'm never happy."

The man's tone said something else entirely. He sounded a little lighter, so maybe he was finally making inroads regarding his relationship with his kids.

"So why are you calling?" Derek asked as he walked into the lobby. He nodded at Mrs. Walsh seated behind the reception desk and pushed open the glass doors. "If you'll have a report from Forbes and contracts for me."

"This is about your father."

Derek felt a chill dance over his skin despite the heat of the May afternoon. "What about him?"

He wasn't even certain how Bill knew Eddie, but if his father was involved this call couldn't bring any good news.

"He came to see me, Derek."

Derek lifted his chin in idle greeting to Oliver and Tammy as they left the Sales Center, keeping to the far corner of the covered porch. "What the hell did he want?"

Bill snorted. "He's a piece of work, your father. All flash and polish, but I'm sorry to say I didn't like him."

"It's the first time you've met him?"

"Son, I wouldn't have any sort of relationship with the family of one of my people without their knowing it."

Derek ran a hand over his face. "What did he have to say."

"He was looking for you. Played it up as wanting to reconnect with his son. He might be able to fool some of the people with that line but not me. I've been working on that very goal myself and I can recognize when someone's being sincere. He wasn't."

Derek's throat tightened. "Did he ask about my mother?"

"He said he'd heard she was living with you in Cypress."

"Fuck. Sorry. I didn't want him to know that."

"He already knew. Maybe your mother let it slip a couple of months ago that you were taking the job?"

"That's possible. My sister said she met for coffee with Eddie a couple of weeks ago."

"I think he might be headed down there, Derek. I wanted to give you a head's up."

This was something Derek didn't need right now. He was navigating his own way in Cypress, in his relationships, and now

249

he had to deal with Eddie?

"Thank you for telling me."

"I'll say it again, son. I don't like him. You get me on the horn if you need anything from me."

Derek felt his eyes prick with tears. Bill had his back. Like a real father would. "Thank you. I will."

"I'll be coming down in a few weeks," Bill said. "For Memorial Day."

"For the festival?"

"Cypress seems to always have a festival, but I want to see the grandkids and get in some golf. Play a round or two with me?"

"Sounds good."

"Take care of yourself, Derek."

It was the warmest, fuzziest good bye he'd ever heard from Bill. He wasn't surprised when the call disconnected. Bill wasn't one for platitudes.

Derek clenched his phone in his fist. Fucking Eddie. What the fuck was he thinking, going to Bill Chapman? Bill had seen right through his bullshit, though. Derek shouldn't have expected any less from his old boss.

He had to see his mother. Warn her that Eddie was asking

around. Angling for some sort of preferential treatment, because that was the way he rolled.

"Fuck," he said again.

Sending crushed shells and gravel spinning, he pulled out of the parking lot and headed for home.

***

Bree stared at her phone, her palms sweating as she studied Derek's text.

Will I see you tonight?

Oh, would he? She didn't dare. It had been rough enough, gazing at him at the meeting this afternoon. Those graceful fingers of his, tapping on his tablet. Those compelling eyes, laser focused on Mr. Forbes and Eli as they laid out the expansive plans for the east side of the property. With her feelings so messed up right now, though? She didn't trust herself around him tonight.

She might gush and confess her undying love, which was something neither one of them wanted. Derek might have asked where they were going. What was this between them? He didn't really want to know, did he? Any guy would take what they had for what it was. Amazing sex and personalities that just…meshed. They were so well-suited to each other, she knew she would somehow mess it up. Somehow become the ice queen she'd been in the past. That had turned guys off faster than losing access to their trust funds.

Busy tonight.

The response was short and way too vague, but she couldn't admit the real reason. Not in a text, at the very least. Holding her breath, she waited for Derek to respond. It took a few minutes but a sad little *okay* showed up on her phone.

Tossing her phone on the couch beside her, she crossed her arms. She wanted to see him. She was busy. That was true. She had notes to review from today's meeting and new scheduling to review for tomorrow. Fridays were busy at the Sales Center. Nearly as busy as Mondays. Still.

She'd told Jessie she would meet her and Noah for a drink tonight, in part to celebrate the big launch. She'd bowed out of that, too. She'd been afraid of running into Derek.

"Idiot."

She stood and went to the fridge, pulling out one of the bottles of wine Derek had brought over last week. This was a nice, crisp white and just what she needed. Taking down one lonely wineglass from the cabinet, she poured herself a drink and returned to the couch.

Her phone was silent beside her. The screen was dark. Yet it was mocking her. Daring her to put on her big girl panties and call Derek. She was in control of her own reactions, wasn't she? She wasn't a silly coed with her first crush. She wasn't a tired debutant with yet another boring fix-up. No. She was Bree James. Self-made woman, sort of, and in charge of her own life. Taking a big swallow of the wine, she set the glass down on the coffee table and picked her phone up again.

"Don't be silly, Bree," she told herself. "Just call him."

Before she could change her mind, she tapped on his number and made the call.

"Bree."

His voice was different. A little strained.

"Derek, is everything all right?"

"I thought you were busy."

There was no accusation in his tone but her cheeks burned anyway.

"I'm not too busy to see you," she admitted in a rush.

"Dinner at the Tavern?"

"How about dinner from the Tavern? I'll order a pizza."

"Sounds good." He was quiet for a beat. "I'm glad you called."

His words warmed her down to her toes. "I'll pick up the pizza and meet you back here?"

"You're not having it delivered?" he asked.

"No. I was supposed to meet Jessie and Noah earlier, so I'll stop by and say a quick hello."

"So you were too busy for them, too." She could almost see his smile. "I guess I don't feel so bad then."

"I'll see you in about a half an hour," she said.

"Good." For a single word, it held a lot of weight.

"Bye."

They disconnected and she headed to the Tavern. It was busy for a Thursday night, so she went up to the counter.

"A large sausage and pepper pizza to go?" she asked.

The kid nodded and she paid for her order.

"That's a lot of pizza for one small girl," Joy said.

"Joy, mind your business."

Joy grinned. "Consider it minded."

Bree smirked at her and walked further into the tavern. There was a man seated at the bar, a tall dark-haired man with an upscale vibe. He was dressed like her father often did. Pricey knit shirt. Pressed trousers. Polished loafers. There was something about him, though. He seemed almost familiar.

"Something to drink?" the bartender asked.

"Nothing, thanks," she told him. "Just waiting for a pizza order."

The bartender nodded and walked further down the bar. The guy, who looked to be about her father's age too, eyed her. She didn't like the way he leered at her, and she marveled that he could make her feel dirty without even speaking a word.

"You should tell your boyfriend to take you to dinner," the guy said.

Bree leaned away from him. She knew he was fishing for information, but he really should cut bait. "I'm bringing dinner home to my boyfriend, actually."

"That's a shame." He turned to face her fully, leaning one elbow on the bar. "I hope he knows just how lucky he is."

Who the heck was this guy? Without answering him, she gave him a tight smile and turned back toward the dining area. Jessie spotted her. She waved and Bree all but ran over to their table.

"What's with the bar fly?" she asked as she joined them.

"The leering dressy guy?" Jessie asked. "Yeah, I saw him checking you out when you came in."

Bree shuddered. "Yuck."

"I thought you couldn't come out tonight, Bree?" Jessie asked.

"I was going to review my notes from the meeting today, actually."

"And now you're ordering a pizza." Jessie narrowed her eyes as a smile played over her lips. "Interesting."

Bree waved a hand. "Don't start with me, Pixie."

Jessie and Noah both laughed at that. Bree heard her name and walked back to the counter to pick up her order. She could feel the older man at the bar watching her and resisted the urge to flip him off. Apparently her mother's repeated training in the social graces still stuck. Margaret James would be proud.

She was just walking into her kitchen from the garage as her front doorbell rang. Her heart did that little skip as she set the pizza box on the tall counter. She opened the door to find Derek standing on the front porch, his hands in his pockets.

"Hey, Bree."

Even as she silently called herself a giant idiot, she wrapped her arms around his neck and kissed him. He froze for a second, and then his arms encircled her. He felt so good. Solid. Real.

Leaning back, she looked up at him. His eyes were dark

and his smile soft.

"Still busy?" he teased.

"Watch it, Due Diligence."

Laughing, they went into the kitchen together.

She loved him. His kisses and his smiles. She wouldn't admit that to anyone, though. Least of all Derek. In his words, she'd break on the cross-examination.

Chapter 19

As Derek left the Sales Center late Friday afternoon, he came to a halt on the steps. What a way to end an otherwise perfect day. He'd spent the night with Bree, or a few mind-blowing hours anyway, and had a productive day at work today. He had his whole weekend ahead of him, to spend with Bree and to look after his mother. But now? Now the day threatened to go to hell in a skiff.

There he stood. Edward Stone, esquire. Or, as he would think of him now given how he was dressed. He must have just come from the Clubhouse after playing a few rounds. Here he was. The devil in golf pants.

"Hello, Derek."

"What are you doing here, Eddie?"

Eddie smiled, that slick expression that masked the bastard within. "Can't a father come to see his son in his new digs?"

Derek stepped closer, breathing in through his nose and slowly letting it out. "What are you doing here?" he asked again.

"I'm here for a visit, son."

His use of the word had the exact opposite effect Bill's had just yesterday. No warm and fuzzy. No pride or admiration. Eddie elicited none of those things and never had.

Derek looked around in the general area and saw that no one from work was around at the moment. "Don't make me file that restraining order, Eddie."

Eddie glowered at him. "Is that a threat, Derek?"

"It's a promise. I won't let you talk to Mom again."

"Fine," his father snapped. His expression smoothed in an instant. "I think I like this Cypress Corners. It's not what I expected."

Derek gave a short, dismissive nod. His mother had said something similar the other day but Eddie made it sound like he found the place lacking. Good. Maybe he'd get the hell out all the quicker.

"Great golf course," Eddie went on. "Just played a round with some guys from Tampa."

"When are you leaving?"

"Is that any way to speak to your father?"

Derek wasn't going to get into this now. "Where are you staying, then?"

"I wouldn't expect you to invite me to stay with you."

No fucking way. "Damn straight."

"I have a room at the Cypress Inn."

"Enjoy your stay."

Derek opened his car door, bracing himself as he heard Eddie's footsteps behind him on the crushed shells.

"I'll see you around, Derek."

He faced his father again, trying a different tack. "How long are you staying, Eddie?"

"I'm not sure. I arrived yesterday, actually. Ate dinner in the tavern last night. Saw a lovely girl there. Stacked. Blond. Leggy."

Derek's skin prickled but he kept his mouth closed tight.

"I happened to speak to a young couple eating dinner there, too," Eddie added. "It seems they're friends of yours. Nate and Jessica?"

He must have meant Noah and Jessie. Derek grunted in answer.

"Yes, they said the pretty young thing with the long blond hair is seeing you." Eddie winked. "Imagine my surprise."

Derek's hands fisted. "So help me, Eddie."

"How did you land a girl like that, son? She's pretty, but there's something else. She looks like our kind of people. Not the type of woman you usually go for."

Derek's shoulders tightened. "Our kind of people?"

"Quality, Derek. You know. Like our friends back in

Boston."

Bree was worlds better than any of his father's friends back in Boston. She was everything.

"Don't talk about her."

His father's brows rose. "Then it's true."

Derek's lips thinned. "You have never had anything to do with me or my life, Eddie. Don't start now."

"How the hell did you hook up with her? Let me guess. She just fell in your lap. You're floating again, with her along for the short ride."

"What?"

"You can't keep her, you know. She's way out of your league."

"Fuck you," Derek growled.

"Easy, son. You see, that was your problem. From when you were a snot-nosed little pussy. You lack determination. Backbone." He snorted. "Balls."

Derek dragged his fingers through his hair as he took in another deep breath. "I'm not going to play this game with you. Not now. Not ever."

"Mark my words, Derek. She'll realize you're just not worth it."

The words struck deep. He didn't care about Eddie's opinion of him. Not in years. What he said about Bree, though? No. He couldn't think about that right now.

"When are you leaving?" he asked his father.

"My stay is open-ended. You see, I have partners at the firm to look after my concerns."

This was another dig at Derek's choices. But as he'd never wanted to even clerk for his father he let it roll off of him like water off a duck's back. He thought of Bree in that second, about what she'd said at her parents' place.

"That's good. You're not going to see Mom."

"I know she's staying with you. Abby told me."

"I can't believe Abby even talked to you."

"She didn't." Eddie shrugged. "Not really. I heard her telling that idiot boss of hers."

"Are you stalking my sister now, too?"

"I'm not a stalker."

Derek held up his hands. "Whatever. This conversation is done. Enjoy your visit."

Derek got in his car and shut the door. "Son-of-a-bitch," he muttered.

Gripping the steering wheel, he held on tight as his heart

pounded. Eddie could work his particular brand of magic without even breaking a sweat. Now he was here in Cypress, damn it.

Derek started the car and drove, spinning crushed shells and gravel as he left the parking lot. He didn't even look to see where the hell Eddie was at the moment. He'd never had any words of encouragement for Derek. The shit he'd said today was nothing new, except for one thing. He wasn't good enough for Bree? Well, hell. That was the one thing Derek had been worried about. She didn't want anyone to know they were dating. She didn't want to talk about where they were going. To define their relationship. Was his father right?

Doubt clawed up the back of his throat. He wasn't good enough. Bree was everything and he was just some guy who didn't even know how to be in a real relationship.

Pulling into the garage, he turned off the engine and just sat there. Tears burned in his eyes so he squeezed them shut. He'd suspected it for weeks now, hadn't he? Bree was better off without him. Without his stunted feelings and closed off emotions. His fucked-up past and lack of sensitivity. He'd talk to her again, and soon. If she insisted they were just fooling around, he would have to end it.

Better to put an end to what they had now before he got in too deep. Eddie was probably right, the bastard. She deserved much better.

He just wasn't worth it.

***

Bree stretched out beside Derek, her bones feeling like molten caramel. Her thoughts were in a muddle, the blame for which she put squarely on his broad shoulders. He'd loved her to within an inch of insanity and now he just lay still beside her like he hadn't moaned and groaned so nicely just a few minutes ago.

"Mmm, nice," she breathed. "That was incredible."

He stiffened, and then let out an audible breath. "We're good together, baby."

She wouldn't look for more in his words. They were good together, not that she had much to compare this to in her adult life.

"I didn't think you'd come over tonight."

"I almost didn't."

His voice sounded stilted now. Flat. Something niggled at the back of her mind. Something troubling. They never spoke of anything deep though, did they? Why would they start now? She sure as heck wasn't going to admit anything.

"Are we doing anything tomorrow?" she asked, eager to put her odd feelings out of her head. "It's Saturday, after all."

"We can do whatever you like."

"What's your mother up to?"

He jerked a little and then brushed his hair off of his brow. "I don't know."

"Derek, what's wrong?"

He turned his head and she gasped at the turmoil in his gaze. "My father's here."

She sat up, dragging the sheets along with her to cover herself. "Here? In Cypress?"

"Yes." He sat up, resting his arms on his sheet-covered knees. "He's been here since Thursday."

"I'm so glad we got together Thursday night."

"I didn't know he was here until today." He ran a hand over the sheet, his fingers clenching and unclenching. "He told me he saw you at the tavern."

Realization struck her. "Ew, he was the guy at the bar."

"What guy?"

"The leering guy who was hitting on me."

Derek cursed softly. "That sounds like Eddie."

"How long is he here?"

265

"He didn't say, but if he thinks he's going to see my mother he's out of his mind."

Bree saw the determination in his expression. Brows drawn together. Lips thinned. She didn't doubt for one second that he would protect his mother to the death. That wasn't a melodramatic thought, either. Not when you were dealing with a scummy guy who abused his wife and children.

"Is he staying at the inn?"

Derek nodded. "Yes. Says his visit is open-ended."

She placed a hand over his fist. "I'm sorry."

Derek stared at their hands, and then looked straight at her. "Thanks, but I'll handle it."

The chill in his voice, in his eyes, was something she hadn't seen in months. "I know you will."

He offered her a tight smile, then slid out of the bed and padded over to the bathroom. Bree nibbled her thumb, sensing some sort of undercurrent to Derek's mood. She was hiding her own stuff, of course. Pushing her feelings way deep down. Would she be as good at keeping that mask in place as she'd seen Derek accomplish? Her heart had nearly broken when she saw the despair in his eyes.

"I'm going to take off," he said as he came back in the

room.

"O-okay." She cleared her throat. "Um, did you want to do something tomorrow?"

"Sure." His voice was clipped, his Boston accent very pronounced. "Text me."

She started to rise but he held out a hand.

"Don't get up," he said.

He placed a knee on the bed and leaned down. His kiss was sweet. Soft. She wanted more but then it was gone.

"Good night," she said softly.

He took a long look at her, his eyes shuttered. "Good night."

She heard his footsteps on the stairs. Over the plank floor. Heard the front door open and close. Heard the latch snick in the doorjamb. He was gone.

Tears burned in her eyes and she dashed her hands over her cheeks. "I'm not going to cry. This is ridiculous."

She put her pajamas on lightning fast and crawled back into bed. She could still smell him. That fresh, hot spicy scent that she'd caught on that very first rainy Monday morning. Her throat tightened. She had to end this. She was way too emotionally involved with a guy who clearly wasn't. He had his family to look after, which would take up his time and his energy.

Saturday morning she rose, rubbing the grit out of her eyes. After brushing her teeth, washing her face and throwing on a pair of yoga pants and a worn FSU T, she headed out to the bakery. Caro Graham was behind the counter, looking fresh and pretty with her bright green apron tied over her baby belly.

"Bree!" Caro tapped the shoulder of her assistant, Jane, and walked around the counter. "I haven't seen you in ages."

They hugged, and Bree smiled. "Look at you. No wonder Eli can hardly stop smiling."

"You know my husband. Eli is always smiling."

Bree thought about how different dark Derek was from his light and bright friend Eli. Eli had his own stuff to work through, according to some of the things Caro had shared with Bree. It was clear that the couple was blissfully happy, though. God, would Bree ever grab on to that kind of happiness if she ever had it? Probably not.

"He's been raving about the lemon lavender scones, too," Bree said. "I think they would be a great way to start my weekend."

Caro nodded, her curly ponytail bouncing. "Sure. Jane, fix

my friend up with a few scones."

"Oh, I only need one for me."

Caro's head jerked back to her. "What? Why?"

Bree shrugged. "It's just me this morning."

"Is it?"

"Caro, what are you talking about?"

Caro lifted her chin toward the entrance. Bree followed her line of vision and saw Derek standing there.

"I thought you would be with Derek today," Caro whispered.

Bree's lips thinned. "Okay, we're dating. I guess everyone knows that. It doesn't mean we're joined at the hip."

Caro laughed. "Where have I heard that before? Oh, yeah. From myself."

"Just the scone, please," Bree said with a shake of her head. "And a large coffee."

Caro patted her arm and hustled behind the counter again. As Bree stepped up to the register she felt him behind her. His heat. His scent. Closing her eyes, she silently prayed for strength.

"Here, let me." Derek handed Caro his credit card. "And add a couple more scones and another coffee, please."

"Derek, you don't have to," Bree began.

He just shook his head. Caro's eyes were wide on them, and so were Jane's, so Bree went over to the condiment station to fix her coffee the way she liked it. Derek drank his black, so he beat her to a round table near the front windows. She joined him, keeping her eyes on the tabletop until she couldn't resist looking at him.

"I didn't think I'd see you today," she said as she stirred her coffee.

He met her gaze, his eyes flat. "I thought you wanted to do something."

"I didn't know if you were going to be free."

He didn't say anything to fill the sudden awkwardness between them. She blew on her coffee and took a sip. God, this was horrible. Not the coffee, which she barely tasted. This whole situation. Her stomach churned and her palms sweat as she caught the chill from him.

"I've been thinking about what you said the other night," he started.

"Oh?"

He nodded. "You're right. This is just what it is."

Her mouth dropped open. "Is it?"

"Yes. I'm sorry if it seemed like I was pushing for more. Neither of us want that."

I do, I do! "I suppose that's true."

"So let's just cool this off a little." He cleared his throat. "If you want to."

"Whatever," she said. "There's no need for any drama."

"No."

They each broke off a piece of their scones and chewed. Bree absently noticed how flaky sweet and unique it was, but if asked at gunpoint to describe the taste she wouldn't be able to. She couldn't taste this either.

"Dinner tonight?" Derek asked after a while.

Bree shrugged. "Maybe."

Her heart seized. Why couldn't she tell him no? For that matter, why couldn't she tell him yes? Tell him that she wanted more than just a casual "whatever" with him?

He stood and she stared up at him. "I'll text you later."

"Take a scone back for your mom, Derek." She folded the bag over the remaining scone and handed it to him.

"Thanks."

He took the bag, his brows knit like he was going to say something more to her. Then he tossed his empty coffee cup in

271

the closest trash can and left the coffee shop.

Bree sat there like an idiot, her tongue stuck to the roof of her mouth. Breaking the scone into little pieces, she stared at the colorful crumbs and cleared her mind of what had just happened. They'd just broken up, hadn't they? It sure as heck felt like it.

"That was brutal," Caro said as she sat in the seat Derek had just vacated. "I'm sorry."

"Sorry for what?"

"Bree, that was chilly."

"It is what it is."

Caro rolled her eyes. "God, I hate that phrase. Did you two break up?"

"No." Bree's eyes watered and she blinked the tears away. "Yes. I think so."

Caro placed a hand on her arm. "Don't lose hope."

"There isn't any to lose, Caro." Bree sniffed. "There never was any hope for a relationship. For either of us."

Caro nodded slowly. "Call me if you want to talk."

Bree sat there alone again, for a long time. Her coffee was cold and her scone a crumbly mess that spilled over the plate's edge onto the tabletop. It was over. Before it could ever really start.

She wouldn't go out to dinner with him tonight. She couldn't hide her feelings for him any longer. So she would just avoid him until they passed.

"Give me your strength, Grandmother," she whispered.

She was going to need it.

Chapter 20

Derek silently cursed himself out on the short drive home. He'd had to give Bree an out. She wasn't up for anything more than what they had right now and how long could they go on half in and half out of a relationship? He sure as hell couldn't. Not any longer.

"It's better this way," he muttered.

He hadn't wanted to break things off. Hell no. He'd wanted to admit that he needed more from her, not less. Last night he'd forced himself to leave her bed. Dragged his sorry ass home to crash on his new sectional.

His mother had fixed him a cup of coffee this morning but he'd wanted to get out of the house. From the concerned expression on his mother's face he'd known she'd guessed it on the first try. He'd fucked up again and was taking the easy way out. Floating, just like Eddie always said he did.

He'd spotted Bree's Mustang parked in front of the bakery and made the snap decision to forego the coffee shop for Eli's wife's place. Bree hadn't been hard to miss in the small bakery. Snug black pants hugging that sweet little butt of hers. Thin maroon T-shirt with all that blond silky hair pulled up in a ponytail. She'd looked bright and happy as she'd talked to Eli's wife. Bright and happy until she'd seen him standing there, anyway.

He parked the Lexus in the garage and sat there for a long minute. Letting out a breath, he grabbed the green paper bag from the bakery and went through to the kitchen.

"Leave," he heard his mother say from the entry. "Now."

He tossed the bag on the counter and hurried toward the front door. Eddie was on the front porch, talking to his mother who stood in the opened doorway. She didn't look upset, just really pissed. He'd never seen her pissed before. It looked good on her.

"Get the fuck away from her," Derek growled.

Eddie turned is head to glare at him. "Derek, you're back." He slipped his hands in the front pockets of his golf pants. "How's your hot little girlfriend?"

Derek heard his mother gasp and he placed a hand on her shoulder. "Mom, are you all right?"

"Yes, Derek." She folded her arms across her chest. "I was just telling your father to leave."

"To leave?" Derek asked. So he hadn't heard her incorrectly.

"Yes," she said. "To leave your house and to leave Cypress

Corners."

A deep frown creased his father's face. "It seems your mother has as little respect for me as you do."

Derek crossed his arms now. "Color me surprised."

Eddie's face twisted in an ugly sneer. "You can both go to Hell, then." He turned to his ex-wife. "You're not getting anything else from me, Susan."

"I already have everything I need." She lifted her chin. "My brilliant son saw to that."

Eddie grumbled. "Yes, my team couldn't find anything at fault with the agreement Derek prepared."

"Praise, Eddie?" Derek scoffed. "A shame it's too little too late. When are you leaving?"

"You think you've bested me. You'll never best me."

"Eddie, you'll never be anything more to me than a minor inconvenience," Derek said. "And if you even think to bother Abby when you get back to Boston, I'll know about it."

Eddie threw up his hands. "Whatever. You'll regret this, Derek. You need me. You're as weak as your mother is."

The sound of a hard slap to the man's cheek was a welcome surprise. His mother got in Eddie's face, a determination there Derek hadn't seen in years. She wore that

276

even better than her anger.

"You won't speak to my son that way. Get out, Eddie. No one wants you here."

"I'll do what I want to," Eddie said. "I talked to the lovely lady who runs the inn, Derek. She also told me about the late nights you had there with your pretty little girlfriend."

Derek knew Eddie was grasping at anything to hurt him but he wouldn't play. "Go. Go back to Boston. If I hear you've done anything to Mom or Abby, Eddie? You can't run fast enough or far enough. Forget about a restraining order. I'll broadcast just what kind of a bastard you are. See if you keep your country club membership and yacht club friends then."

Eddie's eyes widened. "Fine."

He stepped off the porch and trotted to a golf cart parked at the curb. Derek recognized it as one of the few carts used by the inn. So he had apparently schmoozed Mrs. Rollins into letting him borrow it. Derek shut the door tight. Typical Eddie.

"Oh, Derek." His mother wrapped her arms around his waist. She was trembling and her voice sounded a little hoarse. "I'm so sorry I didn't listen to you sooner."

He held her close, resting his chin on the top of her head. "It's all right, Mom."

"He's such a…prick."

Derek felt a laugh bubble up in his chest. She really was picking up some of Abby's habits. "Yes, he is."

She sniffled, and then held herself away from him. "He's wrong, you know." She swiped at her eyes. "You're not weak."

"Thanks, Mom."

She squeezed his biceps. "You're strong, and not just in muscle."

"You're strong too, you know."

She lifted her chin. "I'm starting to believe that." She grinned. "It felt really good to smack your father across the face."

"It felt good to see it."

Patting his arms, she stepped away from him. "Now what was that fool saying about Bree?"

Derek shrugged. "Nothing that matters."

Her eyes narrowed. "It matters to you. I can tell."

"It was just his usual brand of crap, Mom."

She urged him toward the kitchen. "Did you see Bree this morning?"

"I did."

"And how did you leave things?"

"What things?"

"Things between you, my son." She clicked her tongue. "I tell you, I was stunned when you came home last night."

His cheeks heated a little but he covered by reaching for the bakery bag. "I brought you a lemon lavender scone. It's something new from the bakery."

She opened the bag and breathed in the contents. "Oh, that smells delicious!" She withdrew the pastry and set it on a napkin. "You didn't get yourself one?"

"I ate mine there."

"With Bree?"

"Yes." He sat down on one of the barstools Bree had helped him choose. "With Bree. But I think that's over."

"It's over?" She planted herself on the stool next to him. "Wait. You *think* it's over? Derek, that doesn't make sense."

"I've never had a relationship, Mom. Ever."

She tilted her head to one side. "Are you saying that you've never...?"

He leveled a look at her. "No. Come on. I've never had a girlfriend, though."

"And now you have Bree."

"No. Now I don't have Bree."

"You do! Derek, I saw the way she is around you. The way you were with her that night at dinner. It's clear you're made for each other."

Derek shook his head. "She isn't in this for the long haul. For something real."

"She told you that?"

"Yes. No. Not exactly but we've just been floating."

She winced. "Ugh, don't use that word. That's an Eddie word, and it's ugly."

"It is what it is, Mom. I think it's time to step back and give her the space she clearly wants."

"Did you tell her you love her."

His mouth dropped open. "What?"

"You love her." She shook her head. "Derek, you love her. That's clear. I've never seen you care about whether or not a woman was in it for *real*."

He blinked as his mind flashed through the past few weeks with Bree. It was different. Better. Very real. "I love her?"

His mother laughed softly. "Are you asking me or yourself?"

"Neither. I love her. Damn, I didn't see this coming."

"The question now, dear son, is what are you going to do

about it?"

That was the million dollar question, wasn't it? He might not know if Bree loved him but he sure as hell loved her. He just had to figure out the best way to show her what they could really be to each other.

Forever.

***

Bree's front doorbell rang around seven o'clock in the evening. She hadn't heard from Derek at all since seeing him at the bakery, let alone get any texts about meeting him for dinner tonight. So it was leftover pizza and a smoothie for her. A half healthy, half not-so-healthy dinner, but it was fine. She wouldn't let it bother her. It was what it was.

"Ick, that *is* a stupid saying." Peering through the peephole she was shocked to see her father standing on her porch. Opening the door, she peered at him. "Dad?"

"Hi, honey."

She looked over his shoulder but he appeared to be alone. "Why are you here? And where's Mom?"

"Your mother had a club dinner tonight and, frankly, I just didn't want to go." He winked. "It's really more of a hen party, anyway."

"Come in." She waved him inside and shut the door behind him. "Can I get your something to drink?"

"No thank you." He looked around the great room, the kitchen. "Your house looks different, Sabrina. More lived in."

"I went to Grandmother's storage unit."

His brows shot upward. "You did? Good for you, honey. It's about time."

"Sit, Dad." He settled on the couch and she joined him. "Why are you really here?"

"I wanted to talk to you. To tell you that it doesn't have to be this way."

"What way?"

His eyes, the same blue as hers, narrowed. "You know very well what way. This distance. Your mother doesn't like it. I don't like it."

Bree swallowed. "Distance works for us, Dad. It keeps things civil."

"Civil? Maybe." He leaned forward, placing his hands on his knees. "I want more than that with my only child."

Her lower lip trembled. "Dad."

"Let's put the whole Kip fiasco behind us, Sabrina. He's proven himself to be a snake in the year since his phony proposal."

"Phony?"

"We should have listened to you and not his lies. He's just a trust fund baby with little to occupy himself." He shrugged. "So he lies."

Bree settled back, her mind working through all her father was saying. "Mom agrees with you on this?"

"She does. She's been upset about things between us since the May Day party."

"Why didn't Mom come with you?"

"She's stubborn, Sabrina." He grinned. "A lot like someone else we know and love?"

"Yeah, I can be stubborn."

"And strong. And determined. You're all of those things, honey."

A lump formed in her throat. "Thank you."

His eyes were shiny and, being Arthur James, he stood and walked around the room in an attempt to hide his emotions. "You have a lot of my mother's things here. That lamp. Ah, the hope chest."

"I've only brought in a few things so far," she told him. "Derek brought the chest in from the garage for me."

"Derek Stone. Yes. We enjoyed meeting him."

She didn't say anything to that. She couldn't, so she simply nodded.

"What do you say about coming for dinner, Sabrina? Every few weeks? We would love it."

Bree considered what he was proposing. With her non-relationship with Derek over, and she was pretty sure it was over, what else did she have to do on the weekends?

"We can try that, Dad."

He smiled wider than she'd ever seen. "Good!" He came back to the couch and hugged her. That was also unusual. "Your mother will be so happy."

She closed her eyes and rested her head on his shoulder. "I'm glad." And she was being honest. "Very glad."

"Good." He patted her on the back and released her. "Your mother will make the arrangements. Of course."

Bree smiled. "Of course," she agreed.

"I'll leave you alone now."

"You won't stay for a drink or anything?"

"No, I'm good. It's been a while since I've had the house to myself. Maybe I'll watch something on ESPN. In my underwear."

She laughed. "Lovely image, Dad."

He patted her leg. "Don't get up. I'll see myself out."

"Okay."

He walked over to the front door. "So we'll see you soon, Sabrina? And bring that boyfriend of yours."

"I don't think that will happen."

"What? Why?"

"I think that's over."

"You think it's over? I don't understand."

"We weren't really anything, Dad."

"But you love him."

Her throat tightened again. "I do. How did you know that?"

"It's a father thing, I guess. Things will work out, honey. You'll see." He opened the front door and chuckled. "Sooner than you think, I'll bet."

"Thanks, Dad."

She leaned her head back as the front door closed. Sighing loud and long, she placed an arm over her eyes. Her father's apologies and disclosures weren't expected but very welcome. She would talk to her mother soon, she imagined. And they would make arrangements for a family dinner.

In her mind's eye she pictured the table, exquisitely set.

The food, perfectly prepared. The chairs occupied by only her and her parents. Derek would have been welcome. He would have fit right in.

"That's never going to ever happen," she murmured.

"What's never going to happen?"

She jumped up, turning to see Derek standing in her entry. "Derek!"

"Your father let me in." He stood there, shifting from foot to foot. "I hope that's okay."

She managed to nod. "What do you want?"

"You." He winced. "That's not it. I mean, I do want you but that's not why I'm here."

This was beyond weird. Derek was never flustered and he certainly never misspoke. Words were his thing.

"Derek?"

"I love you, Bree. I'm sorry, but I love you."

Her breath caught. "What?"

He started to pace, dragging his fingers through his hair. "I know we talked about this and you don't want a relationship. I was ready." He stopped and faced her. "I was ready to walk away but I can't."

She brought her hand to her throat, taking in shallow

breaths as she tried to wrap her head around his words. "Derek, what are you saying?"

He came over to her, standing close but not touching her. "I don't want to just float, Bree. I don't want to lose what we have."

"I don't either."

His eyes widened. "What?"

"I don't want to lose this either, Derek." She sucked in a breath. "I love you, too."

He waited a beat, and then grabbed her in his arms. "Ah, Bree. That makes me so happy."

His voice was thick. Emotional. She leaned back and looked into his face. There was no mask there. No coldness. Just raw and wonderful affection heating his eyes and curling his lips at the corners.

"Oh, Derek." Her tears started, and she couldn't stop them if she tried. "I'm so happy."

He brushed a thumb over her cheek. "Don't cry, baby. Don't cry. I might not know just how to do this, but I'm pretty sure you're not supposed to cry."

"How to do what?"

"Commit to this relationship. Make a life together. Be

together forever."

"Forever?"

To her shock he fell to one knee. "Marry me, Bree. I don't have a ring yet but I want to be with you forever."

Her heart danced all around in her chest as she laughed through her tears. "Okay, forever. I can do that. Yes."

He smiled up at her and stood. "We'll be happy. It won't be perfect. I'm sure I'll make mistakes. But we'll be happy."

"I don't want perfect, Derek. I just want you."

He held her close again, his every breath matched to hers. This was what she'd wanted. For weeks now. Derek might not think he was perfect but he was perfect for her. Forever.

Epilogue

Derek sat on the balcony off the master bedroom, a bottle of Sam Adams in his hand. The Adirondack chair was a little hard but the pillows at his back cushioned the wooden slats. It was just past eight o'clock on a Friday, and sunset wasn't far off. The sky was growing darker as the stars began to blink into view.

His feet were bare. His collar was undone and his sleeves and pant cuffs were rolled back. He was rumpled. Comfortable. Totally Cypress Derek.

The day had been a hot one, even for late June. He knew it would only get hotter in the coming weeks, it was Central Florida after all, but he wouldn't trade the heat for the more temperate weather in Boston this time of year. Not for any amount of money, much to Bill's dismay. His old boss and surrogate father had been right after all. Derek had come to Cypress and never gone back.

When Bill had been down for Memorial Day he'd pointed out that forecast with a smile as they'd played their promised round of golf. He'd seemed more comfortable with his kids on that visit too, but Derek still felt that fatherly concern in his direction.

There had been no word from his real father since last month, but he knew better than to think Eddie wouldn't show up again like the bad penny he was. Derek and his mother were braced for him, though. That restraining order he'd prepared was ready to go at any moment.

"I knew I'd find you out here."

He turned his head to find Bree walking toward him, a wineglass in her hand. She wore another worn FSU T-shirt and a pair of denim shorts that showed off her long smooth legs. She kicked off her sneakers and padded over to him.

"Where else would I be?" he asked.

"At my house." She laughed softly, tapping his bottle with her glass. "Helping Abby move in."

He shook his head. "No way. Between you and my mother, I'm sure you had everything handled."

"Oh, we did." She sat down and crossed her ankles. "That was a great idea you had, moving the two of them into my house."

"It was purely mercenary on my part, baby."

"Oh?"

"Mmm-hmm. I wanted to make sure you had no choice but to stay here with me until the wedding."

"You're pretty sneaky," she said. "At least we'll have more room for my grandmother's things. I see another trip to the storage unit in our future."

"Yes." He drained his beer and peeled at the label on the neck of the bottle. "By the way, when is the wedding?"

Bree shrugged and sipped at her wine. "I'm leaving that completely up to my mother."

He didn't see any sign of the strain any conversation about her parents used to contain. It had only been a few weeks since they'd announced their engagement but everyone in their ever-widening circle seemed really happy, her parents especially.

"We're expected for dinner on Sunday," she added.

He groaned dramatically. "Please tell me Kip, Skip and Muffy won't be there."

She laughed. "Not on a bet. It won't be as fun as Rick and Harmony's picnic last week, though."

"Not likely, no." He set his bottle on the plank floor. "We don't have to have the wedding in Orlando, do we?"

"No. In fact, I'd love to have it out at the far lakeshore and then have the reception at the Clubhouse. Jessie and Noah's wedding was just beautiful."

"It doesn't matter to me either way. I just want it done."

She arched a fair eyebrow. "In a hurry there, counselor?"

"Yes. I don't want you to come to your senses."

"I'm afraid you're stuck with me. Lettie is taking credit for this, you know," she went on.

"Why, or do I even want to know?"

"It seems she mentioned me to you months ago, Derek. Put a bug in your ear, or something folksy like that."

Derek smiled. "I think we were fated to be together when you slapped me and I kissed you."

The sky grew darker, the stars brighter, and she set her glass down. "You were such a pain that day."

"I was a dick."

She shook her head and settled herself on his lap, her arms around his neck. "You just hadn't realized what was happening to you." She kissed his cheek. His throat. "What you were getting into."

He settled his hands on her waist. "I'll concede you that point. I wasn't prepared, but I made up for that."

"Mmm." She brought her face to his. "Did you, Due Diligence?"

"That's my job, baby. It's what I do best."

"I like the way you do your research, Derek."

He stood, carrying her through the French doors to his bed. Their bed, now. "Then let me be thorough."

He soon had her panting and sighing, and he loved her completely until they were both satisfied. He held her close after, happier than he'd ever been.

Eddie had been right about one thing. Bree had fallen into his lap. He'd stumbled into a relationship with the most beautiful girl he'd ever known. The girl who would be his wife. The perfect girl for him. His forever.

He would never hold back from her, either. Not his feelings and not his love. He'd sealed his fate that day he'd kissed her.

And he was the lucky son-of-a-bitch who would kiss her forever.

About the Author

JoMarie DeGioia is a bestselling author of Historical and Contemporary Romance. She's known Mickey Mouse from the "inside," has been a copyeditor for her tiny town's newspaper, and a bookseller. A hybrid author, she also writes Young Adult Fantasy/Adventure stories, New Adult Romance and Paranormal Romance. She gets lost in DIY projects around the house and works out plot ideas during long runs. She divides her time between Central Florida and New England.

Discover other books by JoMarie DeGioia

The Bridgewater Brides series, including

The Heir's Treasure

The Viscount's Vixen

The Earl's Beauty

The Gentlemen Undercover series, including

A Hero and a Gentleman

The Shopgirls of Bond Street series, including

That Determined Mister Latham

The Dashing Nobles series, including

More Than Passion

Pride and Fire

Just Perfect

More Than Charming

The Gentlemen Undercover series, including

A Hero and a Gentleman

The Cypress Corners series, including

Finding Harmony

Taming Jake

Loving Cassie

Winning Ben

Showing Jessie

Seeing Shannon (Barefoot Bay Kindle Worlds Novella)

Dreaming Eli

Giving Chase (Barefoot Bay Kindle Worlds Novella)

Kissing Bree

Wishing Joy

The Gifted YA Fantasy/Adventure Trilogy, including

Gifted

Braunachs of the Dell series, including

Luke's Gold

Patrick's Promise

Connect with me online

Get the latest news!

Be a VIP Reader!

Twitter: https://twitter.com/JoMarieDeGioia

Facebook:

https://www.facebook.com/JoMarie.DeGioia.Author

Website: www.jomariedegioia.com